THE SWEETEST PAYBACK

JOHNNY

This is a work of fiction. Names, characters, businesses, places and events are the product of the author's imagination or used fictitiously. Any resemblance to actual events, locales or persons, living or dead, is purely coincidental.

www.johnnynovels.com

Cover by The Innocent Bystanders and based on the original design by Andy Gutowski of 423 Creative

ISBN: 1542750644
ISBN-13: 978-1542750646

OTHER BILLY MACK THRILLERS

THE PERSIAN WALTZ
Volume 1 - Rome

THE OTHER RULE
Volume 2 - London

THE CARDINAL RULE
Volume 3 - Rome

ACKNOWLEDGMENTS

THANK YOU

Caroline Ciaglia for your help, your sage advice and sharp eye -- all invaluable. You helped make the story so much better - again.

Leo Corradini for planting the seed.
Jim Ashley for being a sounding board and providing great advice.

Chris and Cathy for your friendship encouragement and support.
Scot and Yvonne for your friendship, encouragement and support.

My Family for always being there for me.

Andy Gutowski for your influence on the cover. Your creativity amazes me. 423 Creative is the best design, branding and marketing firm out there!

DEDICATION

To my Dad, Tom Mee, who passed away while I was writing this story. Your love, your advice, the life lessons you taught me and the example you set will be greatly missed. I was lucky and blessed to have you as my father. I think of you every day.

CHAPTER 1

Billy Mack stood on the cliff looking down on the Swiss ski village of Klosters six thousand feet below. It was a tranquil Indian summer day but he was on edge, literally and figuratively.

The knot tightening in Mack's stomach was trying to convince him he was being followed.

He knelt on one knee pretending to re-tie his running shoe and surreptitiously glanced back at the metal footing of the cable car station.

There he was again: The man in the blue windbreaker. He was leaning against a fortified steel stanchion and eyeing Mack without looking at him. The man was becoming more brazen, getting closer.

Sunshine shot through an opening in the clouds

hitting the man's face at the perfect angle to spotlight the bane of pockmarks on his cheeks. The man had once suffered from either smallpox or bad acne.

Seeing the man this close persuaded Mack to believe the knot in his gut. He asked himself: why was he here?

~

Four hours ago, Mack had left his chalet and hiked up the *Gotschna*, the mountain hovering over Klosters. An hour into his three-hour hike, he noticed a man wearing a dark blue windbreaker and black baseball cap a hundred meters behind him. If Mack sped up, the man sped up. If Mack slowed, the man slowed. For the rest of the trek up, the man stayed a hundred meters behind.

When Mack reached the top of the mountain, he went for a five-mile run over the catwalks connecting the various ski trails. As he traversed the trails, he repeatedly saw the man in blue windbreaker off in the distance.

There was just enough of a nip in the air for a comfortable run. Mack wrote the sightings off as a coincidence and focused on his running pace.

After his run, Mack hiked over to the restaurant adjacent to the cable car station to have lunch on the wooden deck overlooking the Alps. While Mack was eating, the man in the blue windbreaker strolled onto the deck, glanced at Mack then sat at a table against the far railing and faced him. When Mack looked over, the man turned his head and acted as if he were admiring in the scenic mountain peaks. This happened more than once.

That was when Mack decided not to have a beer for dessert and to head back down the mountain.

~

Mack kept the man in the blue windbreaker in the corner of his eye. He switched legs and pretended to re-tie his other shoe. He glanced back and caught the man staring at him. This time the man didn't turn his head.

Fifty feet to the left was the start of the catwalk winding back down to the village. Mack debated whether to jog down the mountain or ride down on a crowded cable car.

After another glance back, Mack made his decision. He would not jog down the mountain, he would not ride the cable car down – he would *run* back down the mountain and see what happens.

Mack jogged over to the catwalk, stared at the man for a good five seconds then headed down the mountain.

The catwalk widened as he descended. On each switchback, he picked up his pace. A half-mile and ten switchbacks later he was in a full run.

At the last switchback, he glanced up through the trees. The man was fifty-meters behind in a full sprint, his blue windbreaker unzipped and flapping behind him.

Coming into Klosters, Mack crossed the bridge over the *Landquart River* and sprinted up the street. He ducked into the underpass below the railroad tracks and slowed to a walk. He came up on the other side of the tracks to see the man in the blue windbreaker standing in middle of the bridge frantically turning his head left and right.

Mack blended in with the crowd and walked briskly back to his chalet. He *was* being followed.

~

After a long, hot shower, Mack strolled onto the rooftop deck and made his way toward the railing. He scanned the village streets below trying to spot the man in the blue windbreaker, or anyone paying him too much attention. The streets were nearly deserted as folks made their way home for dinner. Either Mack shook off his tail or his pursuer decided it was time to stay out of sight.

Tired from his hike and run, Mack stretched out on the chaise lounge, looked up at the *Gotschna* and let out a sigh. No one should know he was here.

To relax, he concentrated on his breathing. The Alpine air in Switzerland was invigorating and healing, like nowhere else in the world. Mack understood why for hundreds of years, people trekked here to find '*the cure*.'

Mack's concentration was shattered when his phone vibrated and spun on the glass tabletop next to him. When the phone quit dancing, it jingled a different ring tone than the one Mack was accustomed.

He accidentally tapped the wrong icon on his new smart phone then tapped through three screen shots until a green circle appeared.

His firm upgraded his phone to the newest generation and he was still figuring out this new ultra-secure device. The name partners of Mack's Chicago-based firm, Baxter, Israel & Gunn, or "BIG" as it was called on Wall Street, were adamant everyone in the firm be available twenty-four seven, no matter where they were in the world — *just in case*. As such, everyone in the firm was required to carry this new "*un-hack-able*" phone.

Mack didn't care much for the company rule but the firm paid for his phone and its usage so he kept his mouth shut and his phone by his side.

Mack was the firm's troubleshooter. His job was to fix problems and close difficult deals. That meant he had no choice - he was to be available twenty-four seven.

He picked up the phone wondering why anyone at the firm would be calling him on his *compulsory* vacation. On the fourth ring, he hurriedly brought the phone to his ear and hesitantly answered, "Billy Mack."

"Billy, where are you?" Mack recognized his sister Terri's voice. Unfortunately, he also recognized the panic in her voice.

"Switzerland," he answered as he stood and walked back inside the chalet. "What's wrong?"

"Layla is missing."

Layla Rose Giovani was the adopted daughter of Mack's older sister Terri and her husband Hermi. A year ago in London, Layla was an orphan living a life not her own. She was a victim of a worldwide sex trafficking ring run by Lev Sokolov, a Russian gangster now serving a life sentence, thanks to Billy Mack. After Mack extracted Layla from Sokolov's clutches, he arranged for his sister and brother-in-law to adopt Layla, then fifteen... going on forty.

To expedite Layla's adoption, Mack called in every favor and pulled every string he could in England and America.

From the weekly accounts Mack received from his sister, Layla had adapted quickly to her new life. She loved Miami, thrived in high school and was dating the captain of the baseball team.

Mack looked at his watch. It was six p.m. in Klosters, meaning it was noon in Miami. He asked, "Are you sure? How long has she been missing?"

"Of course I'm sure," Terri yelled into the phone. She sniffed back a tear. "I'm sorry. We had her sixteenth birthday party yesterday..." There was a brief silence. "She was hoping you'd surprise her." Terri waited for Mack to answer. No answer Mack could give would absolve him from missing Layla's sixteenth birthday party. That didn't matter right now.

When he didn't answer she continued, "After the party, she went with some friends into Coconut Grove. Billy, she never came home."

He asked, "Have you talked with her friends? Maybe she stayed the night with one of them?"

"She would have called to tell us. Anyway, I called all her friends last night and spoke with everyone who went with her to the Grove except her best friend, Holly. Then I called the police. They took my information but said I had to wait twenty-four hours before she's considered missing."

"Why didn't you speak with Holly?"

"She wasn't home when I called and her mother promised to call when Holly came home. Holly never came home. That's why I'm calling you."

"Is Holly missing too?"

"She was until a cop found her in a dumpster behind a Cuban restaurant. The police called me for a description of Layla, thinking it might be her. When they gave the description of the girl, I knew it was Holly."

"Is Holly... dead?"

"No, Holly was unconscious with a huge welt on the back of her head. She's in the hospital for observation."

"Has she come to?"

"Yes and no. She goes in and out. It didn't matter. I rushed over to the hospital and talked with her."

Terri sucked in a deep breath to keep from crying.

"Holly remembers leaving the café just before midnight. They were going home. The next thing she remembered was waking up in dumpster while two cops were pulling her out. She threw up on one of the cops."

"Where did they find Holly?"

"I told you, in a dumpster."

"No, on what street, give me the address."

"In Coconut Grove at the corner of Main Highway and Charles Avenue, only two blocks from the café." Terri sniffed back tears. "I have a terrible feeling she's been kidnapped."

Mack heard his sister weeping. He stared out the window at the Alps waiting for her to collect herself.

"I don't know what to do, Billy. I can't just sit here," Terri finally said, her voice cracking at the end.

"Has anybody contacted you with any demands?"

"Nobody," Terri answered, her voice a couple octaves higher. "Why would anybody kidnap Layla?"

Mack stared up at the cable car station sitting atop the *Gotschna.* He thought about the man in the blue windbreaker. Unable to make a connection to Layla, he dismissed the thought.

Next, he organized his thoughts starting with names to contact.

He said, "Let me make some calls. If you hear from Layla or from whoever took her... *if someone took her,* text me then call me. Stay positive."

"I, I will. Oh my God Billy, I'm scared."

"Where's Hermi?" Mack asked to get her mind off Layla.

"He's out back keeping himself busy. I can hear the mower going back and forth."

"Have him wait inside with you. If you get a ransom call, or any call, put the phone on speaker so you both can hear. Two ears are better than one when you're recounting to the police what was said."

Mack hung up and paced the floor.

Mack prioritized the names to call in his head. Three people stood out. He didn't know exactly what he would say but wanted them to know the situation and that he may need their help. Ray Gunn, one of the name partners of BIG, would be his first call. In a previous life, Gunn worked in the shadows of American intelligence.

His second call would be to Nimesh, once the NSA's top white-hat hacker.

His last call would be to his uncle Ken, better known as Ken Cardinal Kauftheil. Uncle Ken was recuperating at the Vatican Hospital. Mack would ask him to make a discreet, *just-in-case* call then say a prayer for Layla.

Mack walked back out on the deck. The September sun was nestled against the mountain peaks. He shivered but it wasn't from the cool air of the setting sun.

He tapped Gunn's contact number.

"Why are you calling?" Gunn answered, half joking. "You're on vacation so this better be a *just-in-case* call."

"I have a problem, Ray and need your help."

"Let me close my door."

Mack heard Gunn humming a concerned '*hmm hmmm hmmmmm*' then his door close.

"What's up, Billy?"

"Layla is missing." Mack repeated his sister's words verbatim.

Mack could hear Gunn thinking. He had a habit of softly clicking his tongue against the roof of his mouth when he mulled something over. It was nearly inaudible but Mack, knowing Gunn as well as he did, clearly heard.

Gunn finally spoke. He asked, "You say her friend was left in a dumpster and is now in the hospital for observation?"

"That's what Terri said."

"Where exactly was Layla when she was taken?"

"She was in Coconut Grove, near the corner of Main Highway and Charles Avenue. It's by the Taurus Bar, your old hangout," Mack said.

"That's usually a busy area."

"She just turned sixteen, Ray."

There was a long silence before Gunn said, "This is no random abduction. This was a professional job. If it were random, it would be some pedophile acting alone and away from a busy street. Plus, those perverts never approach two girls and only take one."

"Why would pros target Layla?"

"Good question, Billy. Sit tight and let me make a couple two, three calls and get back to you."

~

CHAPTER 2

To take his mind off Layla, Mack snatched a blue can of *Puntigamer* beer from the refrigerator knowing it was sacrilegious to drink Austrian beer in Switzerland.

He took a swig and caught his reflection in the mirrored glass on the microwave. He brushed back his thick brown hair and scrutinized his appearance. His black t-shirt and khakis hung loosely on his athletically thin frame. He'd lost weight over the last month and was lighter than his playing days as the third baseman for the Chicago White Sox. If he didn't eat three meals a day, he lost weight. He walked out of the kitchen reminding himself to eat regularly. He'd need the energy to find Layla.

He went back out on the deck and sat in a lounge

chair. The sun was dropping slowly behind the mountains, preparing to end the day.

He stared blankly at the sunset wondering why a professional would kidnap Layla. It didn't make any sense.

He pictured Layla when she first came into his life. She was a frightened fifteen year-old on the run and looking for a guardian angel. She stumbled into Mack and latched on. He would never let go.

The vibration in his pocket startled him, again. It brought him back to the here and now. He fished the phone from his pocket. The screen read: Ray Gunn.

"Alright Billy, I have a close friend on his way to your sister's house. He will stay with her until we find Layla."

"Who is it? I'll call my sister and let her know."

"His name is John Kessler. He's the best person for this situation. We played football together in college. He was an All-American linebacker and played in the NFL until he blew an ankle. He's tall, about six-three and except for his ankle, could still play in the NFL. The last time I saw him his hair was long, below his shoulders. I heard, though, he now shaves his head. He's a chameleon, which is quite a feat for anyone as big as him. You're in good hands, because he's the best in the business at finding and rescuing people. I trust him with my life, so can you."

"Is he a cop?"

"Umm, yeah... let's say he is. He's already contacted a Miami-Dade detective he knows. Kessler is coordinating with him. The detective is reviewing the street cams in

Coconut Grove to see if the abduction was caught on camera. He's starting with nearby traffic cams looking for anything suspicious then will expand his search."

Prior to co-founding BIG Investments, Ray Gunn worked in one of the intelligence agencies. Which one, Mack didn't know but after meeting some of Gunn's *visitors* in Chicago, he was certain it was the group within the agency that worked in the shadows, chasing shadows.

"Thanks Ray."

"Don't thank me yet, we have a lot of work to do. I want you to call Nimesh at Mira Labs."

"He was my next call."

"Give him a few minutes. He's talking to um... a colleague, for lack of a better word. Her name is Caroline and she works for an organization in Einsiedeln. It's a town near the south end of Lake Zürich."

"I'm familiar with Einsiedeln and what they are capable of doing. Does Caroline have a last name?"

"Yes."

Mack waited until he realized Gunn was done answering. "You're not going to tell me, are you?"

"It's need to know and you don't."

"What does Caroline do?"

"Let's say she's a cop too, a global cop that dispenses a particular brand of law and order. She has very few constraints and a dangerous reach. Dangerous for the bad guys, that is. Nimesh will explain how she can help."

Mack said, "I hope this will all be for naught and I get a call telling me Layla is home safe and sound."

"Don't wait by the phone for that call."

Mack hung up and downed the rest of his beer. He

trudged back into the kitchen for another. He popped open the can, went back out to the deck and slumped back down in the chaise lounge. He put his feet up and let out a frustrating groan then thought about what to tell Nimesh.

He organized his thoughts and called Mira Labs. He was told Nimesh was out running and would be back in an hour — that is if he was on one of his short runs. Mack knew never to interrupt Nimesh when he's on a run. It was when he cleared his head and did his best thinking. He'd call back in an hour.

He looked up at the mountain peak hovering over the village and asked, "Why the hell would someone abduct a sixteen-year old girl?" He kept his eyes on the peak expecting the mountain to answer him.

~

As dusk settled over Klosters, Mack couldn't sit idly any longer. He needed to move, clear his head and concentrate on finding Layla. He strolled back inside and put his half-finished beer back in the refrigerator. He'd finish it when he returned.

Out on the street, he thought about the man in he blue windbreaker. He twisted right and left seeing nothing but empty streets.

The lights of the *Berghaus Alpinrösli*, a traditional Swiss restaurant halfway up the mountain, flickered in the twilight. It was a thirty-minute walk up but only a fifteen-minute walk back down. Mack needed to calm down before he ate something and the climb would relax him. He cut through a number of alleys and small streets to make sure he wasn't being followed.

As he started up the mountain, his steps were heavy. Halfway to the restaurant he stopped to call Nimesh in Washington DC. Below him, the lights of the small mountain town began to twinkle as they came to life.

"Mira Labs. How may I direct your call?"

"Hi JaNessa, it's Billy Mack again. Is Nimesh-"

JaNessa cut him off. "He's expecting your call Billy. I'll connect you."

Mack heard two clicks and wondered if Nimesh was recording the call or if he recorded all calls.

Nimesh was born in Chennai, India but raised in Brooklyn. He graduated top of his class at M.I.T. with million dollar offers from every high-tech firm in Silicon Valley. He turned his back on corporate life and joined the Green Berets. After ten years as a reconnaissance specialist and four tours in Afghanistan and Iraq, the NSA recruited him. Three years later, frustrated with the bureaucracy and needing a change, he retired. He dyed his hair blonde and set out on his own. He opened Mira Labs, a 'computer consulting' firm with venture funding by BIG, spearheaded by Ray Gunn. No one knows Nimesh's last name or if he even has one. Mack was convinced Nimesh electronically erased his past but couldn't prove it in a court of law.

"Hey Billy, it's Nimesh. I'm sorry about Layla. I will do everything possible to help find her. You have the full resources of Mira Labs at your beck and call. I've already spoken with John Kessler and he connected me with a Miami-Dade detective named Jamie Coppola. I have access to all street cams in Miami and Coppola will be canvassing the local establishments for any security video."

"Thanks Nims, I knew I could count on you. I don't know much right now and it's driving me nuts. Maybe it'll help me if I can pick your brain."

"I understand you're in Klosters for some R and R." Nimesh said to as a way to calm Mack, get him to think straight.

"I was until my sister called. I can't stay here... unless Layla is back home safe and sound before morning."

"If that call doesn't come by morning, I want you to drive to Einsiedeln and meet with a woman named Caroline. She's expecting you. She has access," Nimesh paused, "legal and political access to people and systems I don't. She's up to speed on the situation."

"What about Susan Baisley? She helped with my problem in Vienna."

"Susan's a cryptologist, the best. But Caroline is better for handling issues like this. She a fixer, kind of like a *consigliore*, if you know what I mean."

"She's connected?"

"To the power elite. If they have a problem, she's their solution."

"Tell me about her so I know what to expect."

"I can't. You don't have the security clearance. Let's leave it at that. She'll fill you in on what you need to know. Sorry, those are the rules."

"What's she like?"

"They say there are two types of women in this world and she's neither of them. She marches to the beat of her own drum. She's the smartest person you'll ever meet. She's British, speaks a dozen languages fluently and is conversant in five more. She's a computer genius, reads a book a day and, surprisingly, has common sense. She's a looker too. Keith Richards and Mick Jagger once fought over her. She nearly broke up the Stones. That didn't matter. She turned them both down, said they were too *establishment* for her, meaning too old. Finally, she has a righteous ethical streak and the abduction of a sixteen year-old girl, a British girl no less, will push her into overdrive."

"I'll be at her office at seven."

"She'll be there at eleven. She's finishing up an undercover assignment and is unable to talk so don't call."

"How did you get a hold of her?"

"Don't ask a question I can't answer."

Mack grinned at Nimesh saying 'can't' instead of 'won't.'

Nimesh said, "A little word to the wise before you meet her: she has an eidetic memory down to the smallest details." He paused then said, "I've already told you more than I should."

Mack looked up at the restaurant on the side of the mountain and wondered if he should head to Einsiedeln now.

"Thanks for the head's up, Nims but we're wasting valuable time."

"What can I say? She's on her way back to Switzerland and lands in the morning. I've sent her your details. When you see her, don't be surprised if she already has a few ideas or some leads. Try to relax and get some rest."

Mack knew Nimesh was right — he always was. "Nims, let me pick your big brain. Any idea who would take Layla?"

"There are only two names that come to mind. Both names go back to Layla's time in London."

"Lev Sokolov and J Otis Weil?" Mack said, gritting his teeth.

"She was Sokolov's top money maker in London and that made him my initial guess. But, I checked with a contact in Britain and he's still in prison."

"He could have arranged the abduction from behind bars," Mack said.

"No, Sokolov has dementia and wanders the prison speaking in Russian. He has no idea where he is. He thinks he's Khrushchev and is in a gulag with Stalin and Lenin. He marches around demanding to be returned to the Kremlin."

"That leaves J Otis. Why would that weasel want Layla?"

"If you knew how a weasel thought, he'd no longer be a weasel."

"Is that a Chinese proverb?"

"It's a Nimesh proverb, learned from experience. Expect the unexpected when dealing with weasels."

Mack looked up at the restaurant again. He decided he'd head up, have a schnitzel with fries then head back down, check his computer and finish his Puntigamer beer. He planned to leave for Einsiedeln at six in the morning.

"Why would J Otis be involved?" Nimesh asked,

interrupting Mack's thoughts.

"Most likely payback for something."

"You once told me that J Otis lives by the code 'don't get mad, get even.' If he's involved, why does he want to get even? Think about that."

Mack thanked Nimesh and hung up.

As he trudged up the hill, he tried to come up with other names that made sense — someone with a connection to Layla or a reason to kidnap her.

Except for J Otis Weil, he couldn't come up with a single name.

His gut told him J Otis didn't have the stones do this alone. If he's involved, somebody else was doing his dirty work.

~

CHAPTER 3

Mack jumped out of bed at five-thirty, a half-hour before his alarm was set to go off. He instinctively went for his workout gear: running shorts, running shoes and phone. He realized what he was doing and jammed the gear into his travel bag. He walked to the window and fixed his gaze on the Big Dipper hanging over the mountain peaks.

Along the horizon, a blue hue began to encroach on the night sky and he gazed at the stars as they disappeared.

His phone beeped twice telling him he had a text message. It was from Nimesh:

A go for 11 - Be on time

Mack's phone showed the time as six a.m. He'd been staring at the dawn sky for nearly thirty minutes thinking about Layla and what she must be going through.

He shaved, showered and was in his rented Audi in ten minutes. He drove down the mountain exceeding the speed limit but not fast enough to wake the local cops from their slumber. He drove in silence. When he reached the autobahn, he kept the car at the speed limit to avoid triggering the numerous speed cameras lining the road.

Over the rhythmic drone of the engine, Mack recalled the exact moment Layla came into his life.

While working in London in what now seemed like a lifetime ago, Mack was framed for two brutal murders. In order to uncover the truth and identify the real killer, Mack was forced to go underground. While on the run to clear his name, he holed up in a seedy, *don't-ask* hotel in south London. After locking the door and securing the room, he heard a muffled scrape inside the closet and found Layla hiding there. He cringed when he learned of Layla's past. Before her thirteenth birthday, Layla was sold to Lev Sokolov, a Russian gangster controlling the sex trade in London. One night, she witnessed Sokolov slit a man's throat then locked eyes with him. Knowing she was next, she slipped through the clutches of his goons and went on the run. She squirreled her way into the seedy hotel and hid in the closet. Mack remembered his first impression of Layla: An innocent beauty belying a hard life.

~

Nearing the Einsiedeln exit, traffic had picked up and Mack was forced to slow down and go with the flow. He tried to relax. He had two hours to go before he met with Caroline. Coming into the tiny town of Schindellegi, he found a small roadside café next to a bright yellow gas station. He strolled into the empty café, ordered a coffee and waited for the morning rush to end.

Mack's phone rang with the caller ID indicating it was Nimesh. He brought the phone to his ear and before he could answer, Nimesh said, "How's the coffee in Schindellegi?"

"How did... never mind." Mack caught himself before he asked Nimesh another question he wouldn't answer. Nimesh had the technology and the capability to track anyone, anytime, anywhere, even if they were off the grid.

"It's good. It's not as good as Vienna but still very good." Mack took a sip of the coffee to confirm his opinion. He knew well enough not to lie to Nimesh. "What do you have for me?"

"I reviewed the street cameras with help from Kessler and Coppola. We have a video of the kidnapping. Two black SUVs surrounded Layla and her friend. Two big goons jumped out. One grabbed Layla in a bear hug while the other threw a black bag over her head. They threw her in the back seat and sped away. While this was going on, a scrawny little guy jumped out of the second SUV. He snuck up on Layla's friend and whacked her in the back of her head with what looked like a blackjack. He caught her before she fell, carried her across the street and threw her into a dumpster. He was unusually strong for such a little guy."

"Can you identify any of them?"

"Not yet, but we did our homework on the SUVs involved, both stolen. I tracked them through the city of Miami to the airport. They disappeared into a parking garage. There they switched cars and drove out to the private terminal."

"Why would they switch cars?"

"That's what pros do. We have video from the tarmac outside the hangers of the fixed based operators. We think we have something."

"Tell me."

"There were six private jets leaving Miami International Airport yesterday. Three were golfing charters flying to Scotland; two were for a wedding party in Antigua. The passenger manifests on those five flights checked out. The remaining aircraft had a flight plan filed for Moscow. The names on the flight manifest didn't smell right so I ran a check. Unless the passengers were Chicago voters, every name is an alias."

Nimesh paused. Mack listened to the clatter of typing coming through the phone. When it stopped, Nimesh asked, "How do I know?" His question was rhetorical. Mack kept quiet and waited for Nimesh to answer his own question.

Nimesh finally said, "Because if the names weren't aliases, you'd have a plane full of dead people, including two dead pilots."

"Do you have any idea who's on the plane?"

"No, and airport security cameras in Miami didn't

pick up a direct shot of any of the kidnapper's faces. It's as if they knew exactly where the cameras were. There was a small person, female, escorted into the plane by two rather large men, American football player large."

"Can you send me a still of the girl? I may be able to tell if it's Layla."

"I don't need to. I'm positive it's Layla. The plane is registered to a Barcelona-based company, *Oriol Consultoria.* I kept digging and found *Oriol Consultoria* to be a newly established company registered in Panama and owned by JOW Holdings. But that's only a part of the story. The owner of JOW Holdings is Sunden Capital. You know who owns Sunden."

Mack squirmed in the booth with his coffee cup cradled tightly in his left hand. If he squeezed harder, the cup would shatter. He sniffed then said, "J Otis Weil."

"The plane left Miami at one o'clock in the morning. As I said, its original flight plan was for Moscow. While in flight, the pilot changed its destination. It arrived yesterday in Barcelona at one o'clock in the afternoon, Barcelona time."

"Do you have anything for me in Barcelona?" Mack asked. He finished his hot coffee in one swallow.

"Not yet, but I have a couple calls into people both Ray Gunn and I trust. Caroline has a better network in Spain and will be more helpful. If she can't help you, nobody can."

"I'm heading to her location now. Any advice?"

"So there is no shock when you meet her, let me tell you a few things so you are prepared. She dresses like a combination librarian and lumberjack. For some reason, it works. Also, let her talk and tell you what can and can't be done. Ask any question that comes to mind, no matter how dumb. She considers not asking questions a low intelligence quotient, even below asking stupid questions."

"Thanks Nims, I'm heading over to see her now." Mack ended the call and paid the check.

The sky had clouded up while Mack was inside having coffee. As he pulled onto the two-lane highway, it started to sprinkle. He flicked on his wipers and settled in for the drive to the small city of Einsiedeln.

He glanced in his rearview mirror and saw a car coming up fast, too fast. Ten meters behind him, the car, a navy blue BMW, slowed but kept coming up on him. The driver of the BMW was wearing a blue windbreaker and black cap. Mack recognized his pockmarked face. The BMW kept coming closer.

Up ahead was a long curve in the road. He pushed down on the accelerator hoping to put some distance between him and the BMW. In the middle of the curve, he heard the rev of the BMW's engine. He glanced back to see the headlights disappear below his rear window. He felt the thump of the bumpers colliding before he heard the crunch. Mack's car jolted forward and his head jerked back then forward. He moved his eyes back and forth between the road and the rearview mirror while trying to control the car. Coming around a curve, his speedometer read 125 kilometers per hour.

Mack looked up to see a large truck in his lane bearing down on him. The truck was only thirty meters away and closing fast. The driver was leaning forward with a tight grip on the steering wheel and determination glued on his face. As he neared, a smug grin grew across his lips.

Mack kept his nerves steady. The only way he would win this game of chicken would be to react at the exact right moment and turn the car in the correct direction. Choosing the right moment and direction would be a guess, a lucky guess.

Mack had to trust his reaction time and instincts. As a Major League baseball player, he'd learned to trust these skills. At the plate, a batter had a tenth of a second to react to a pitch. The best hitters didn't think - they reacted. That skill was ingrained in Mack and stayed with him after he left the game.

When the truck was ten meters away, Mack jammed down on the accelerator and cranked the wheel toward the on-coming lane.

The car jerked to the left, clipped the front bumper of the truck and shot across the on-coming lane. Mack clutched the steering wheel so tight his fingers turned white. The car spun three hundred sixty degrees.

There was an opening in the metal guardrail on the other side of the road. Mack's Audi shot across the on-coming lane and through the guardrail opening then across a small tract of grass. He slammed on the brakes and skidded across the wet grass. The car seemed to pick up speed as it approached a steep hill running down to a rock-infested river. The car vaulted over the hill, clipping the tops of four birch trees as it plunged toward the river. Mack's world began to move in slow motion. The trees bent in half and snapped like twigs. The car nosedived and plowed grill first into the river.

The airbag exploded knocking Mack back against his seat. The Audi stood on its grill for what seemed like an eternity. Finally, the car creaked loudly and the back end dropped down into the river with a splash. The rear window exploded and the car alarm pierced the air.

Mack swung the door open and jumped into the river. The glacial water was thigh high and numbed his legs. He grabbed his bag, trudged to the shore and climbed back up the hill to the side of the road. He bent over, rested his hands on his knees and said a prayer. He wiped away the blood running from his nose.

On the far side of the street, the truck was sitting atop the blue BMW with the driver hanging halfway out the front window, bent over the hood. Blood was pumping out a wide gash in his neck. A knife-like shard of glass stuck out of his right eye.

The roof of the blue BMW was crushed down to door level and a fire had ignited inside the car. If the man in the blue windbreaker were alive, it would be a miracle.

Sirens wailed from up the hill in Einsiedeln. Mack was disoriented and walked away from the sirens. He sat on the guardrail and fingered his nose to see if it was broken. He winced at the jolt of pain. He'd been hit a few times in the face by a pitched baseball and that didn't hurt half as much.

~

CHAPTER 4

Nuria Oriol peered around the decrepit apartment wondering why her little shit of a partner wasn't already in Barcelona. She shook her head in disgust before she trudged up the steps. On the third step, her breathing began to labor.

Nuria was short, squat and smoked too much. At the top of the stairs, another coughing fit erupted. Her lungs hurt every time she had one of her fits. The fits were occurring more often, every hour or two. She knew her time on Earth was limited. She wouldn't live to see New Year's Eve. Not that she celebrated anything anymore - after what that bastard did to her.

When her fit subsided, she ran her hands through her shoulder length, salt-and-pepper hair and pulled it into a spiked ponytail. Her gray eyes had only a little life left in them. But enough life to accomplish her final mission: to set things right.

She knocked hard and pushed open the bedroom door. Lying on the single bed, nearly naked and in the fetal position was her prize, her trap to set things right... and her last little girl.

Nacho Ybarra sat on a stool next to the bed guarding the prize. He was a former police detective. His black hair was cut military short and he hadn't shaved in days. He was reading a book, not paying any attention to Layla. When Nuria walked in he looked over at Layla as if she didn't exist.

Layla Rose Giovanni lay motionless on the sagging single bed wearing only her bra and panties. She was thin and tan with full brooding lips and long brown hair. She had two tiny birthmarks in the form of teardrops in the corner of each eye. Her left foot was bruised and swollen from the heavy shackle fastened tightly around her ankle.

Nuria motioned for Nacho to leave the room. He averted his eyes as he made his way across the room. When he closed the door behind him, Nuria strolled over to the bed, sat next to her young prize and gently petted Layla's hair.

"I don't think you know how pretty you are." She caressed Layla's thigh. "My daughter was about your age when she was executed."

Layla knew if she moved, even flinched, she'd be beaten.

Nuria grabbed a handful of Layla's hair and jerked her up to the sitting position. "Your strange little birthmarks make you look like you're always crying. If you cry, I will beat you and give you something to cry about. Do you understand me?"

Layla nodded.

"Good girl," Nuria said then pulled Layla close to her and kissed her firmly on the lips.

Layla cringed and nearly gagged. The woman reeked of stale sweat and cigarettes. It was as if someone shoved Layla's face into a dirty ashtray inside a rancid garbage can.

Nuria released Layla's hair and let her fall back onto the bed. "You and I will be making a call soon and you will keep your mouth shut until I tell you exactly what to say."

Nuria marched to the door, jerked it open then turned and faced Layla. "God, you're beautiful... and you are all mine."

She motioned for Nacho to return. As he passed, she said, "Don't talk to her and nobody goes near her. If you let anyone touch her it will be the last thing you do."

Nacho averted his eyes and nodded feebly.

Nuria bounded down the steps with a wide smile plastered on her face. At the bottom of the stairs, the smile disappeared when another coughing fit erupted. This fit lasted longer than normal. When she finished, she spit blood and green mucus onto the floor.

She lit a cigarette and made her way down the narrow hallway to the sitting room. Her youngest son Jordi, her only living child, sat in a wingback chair with a machine pistol resting on his lap and a demonic smile resting on his lips. He was small with a thin face that never touched a razor blade. He was an exact replica of his father down to the demonic smile. His father, God rest his soul, was also named Jordi.

"Did the call come in yet?" Nuria asked.

Jordi shook his head. "Do you want me to call? They should have the bastard man by now."

She handed Jordi one hundred Euros. "Go get yourself an ice cream. If they are not here in an hour, we make the call."

Jordi pocketed the money and stared out at nothing.

"I don't want an ice cream," he finally said. "I want to go upstairs and play with her? I really like her, mother. Please, can I?"

"Not yet. I told you before, no one touches her until this is over and that son-of-a-bitch is dead. Then we will have our fun."

Nuria walked out, crossed the hall to the kitchen. She flicked her cigarette into the sink and found her bottle of *DYC Whisky* in the cupboard. She unscrewed the cap, sucked down a long swig from the bottle and let the burn slide down her throat.

She cursed herself for drinking Spanish whiskey. She hated the Spanish and spit every time she heard the name Francisco Franco. If only *Euskadi*, the Basque Country, made a decent whiskey. She could make regular drives to her hometown of Bilbao and pick up a couple cases of her *golden medicine* on each trip.

She dropped two ice cubes into a glass and filled it with whiskey. She swirled the ice cubes with her finger for a minute then downed a hefty swallow. She relished the burn in her throat. It took away the pain in her lungs. She lit another cigarette and wondered where her partner was. The little shit had his own plane for Christ's sake. The team should have the bait and he should be on his way here.

She took a long drag on her cigarette, down to the filter then tossed the butt into the sink. She took another swallow of her whiskey.

She pulled her phone from her pocket and punched in the number she knew by heart.

Nuria heard the connection click and didn't wait for an answer. "What the hell is going on? I haven't heard from our man."

"I was about to call you. There was a glitch. Well, more than a glitch. Your man failed and he and his *assistant* are both dead."

"What about the targ... the customer? Where is he?"

"I'm looking into that. Your man tried to kill the *customer*. That was not the plan. If he dies, we have no incentive for the killer to come to Barcelona."

Nuria finished her drink and waited for the burn in her throat to subside.

She said, "I gave the explicit order to keep the *customer* alive. My man fucked up, what can I say." Nuria needed to change the subject before she lost her temper with the little shit. "Where are we?"

"The *customer's* car flew into the river but there was no sign of a body when my people arrived."

"Did they check up and down the river?" Nuria nervously lit another cigarette.

"They had to wait a couple hours for the authorities to clear the road. The car was still in the river and the driver's door was open so he must have made it to shore."

"I thought you had someone there who was connected."

"He's in Switzerland, not Spain. Getting one of those fucking Swiss government officials to talk is impossible. I don't care how much you offer them. I have someone digging around. I will call you as soon as I know something."

"You should be here. If the *customer* has the connections you say then we have to be prepared. Once he knows she's here, he'll muster the resources to swarm Barcelona. That means when we make the call we have to move the girl. Nacho's connection has arranged a few places."

"I don't give a damn where you keep her. But, no one touches a single hair on her pretty little head. I want her in pristine condition when I come for her. After this is over, I'll give you one night with her before I take her with me."

"That was not the deal."

"That deal was predicated on your man capturing Billy Mack in Switzerland, not killing him. That- "

"You gave the name, goddammit. Are you stupid."

J Otis clenched his jaw in frustration. "Don't be paranoid. My phone is secure. What I was going to say was you failed so the deal has changed and I get the girl."

"You haven't held up your side of the bargain either. The murderer is still out there and you've done nothing. Our deal was also contingent on you fulfilling your part. That means Jordi and I get the girl."

"The plan was for fucking Billy Mack to be taken to Barcelona. Then the murderer will be forced to bring my money and we kill two birds with one stone. This is on you."

Nuria didn't have the stamina to argue. "I have another pro on standby." Nuria was not about to tell him who. "She will grab Billy Mack, I promise. She has never failed me. Mack will be in Barcelona on schedule. If my girl is successful, and she will be, I keep the little girl until I die or tire of her. Then you can have her."

"You're promises don't mean shit anymore. You still have to get Mack to Barcelona."

"No matter what, the girl's mine," Nuria said.

"My plane is landing soon. We'll discuss this when I get to the apartment and we make the ransom call."

~

CHAPTER 5

Sitting on the guardrail facing the direction of the sirens coming from up the long hill, Billy Mack didn't see the police car roll to a stop on the wet grass behind him. The officer strolled over to Mack, unsnapped his holster and gripped the handle of his pistol.

An ambulance screamed around the corner and came to an abrupt stop next to the wreckage.

The officer re-snapped his holster and walked Mack over to the ambulance.

Mack climbed in the back of the ambulance and sat. A paramedic started asking him questions in Swiss German.

"I'm sorry, can you speak English?" Mack asked.

"Certainly," the paramedic answered. "Can you tell

me what happened?"

Mack explained what happened as the paramedic tended to his bloody nose, checked him for a concussion, broken bones and internal bleeding.

The officer who walked him to the ambulance was from the *Kantonspolizei*, the state police for the Canton of *Schwyz*. Mack didn't like the look on the cop's face. He glared at Mack as if he were guilty.

After being given a clean bill of health, Mack handed his driver's license to the officer. "I can't explain-"

The officer waved his hand, cutting him off. He read Mack's license and said, "Mr. McMillan, you're coming with me to the station in Einsiedeln." It was not a request. "We'll see what happens from there."

A dark gray Porsche Cayenne SUV rolled to a stop next to the ambulance. The driver had a thin face and a full head of hair, cut military short on the sides. He stepped out and approached the back of the ambulance. He ignored the uniformed officer keeping his eyes on Mack instead. He said, "Thank you, Officer Bauer, I'll take it from here."

"Yes sir, Mr. Hew" *(pronouncing it 'Hev')*. Bauer jumped down onto the asphalt, handed Mack's license to Hew and stomped away shaking his head and mumbling to himself.

"Mr. McMillan, please come with me," Hew said.

"Certainly and Mr. McMillan is my father. Please call me Billy."

Hew stared at Mack with a perplexed look. "Your father?" He read Mack's license again and pointed to the name. "Are you not Mr. McMillan?"

"Sorry, that's an old American joke."

Hew chuckled. "Achh, I understand. I will have to tell that joke next time someone calls me Herr Hew." He grinned at Mack. "Please retrieve your bag and get in the car so we can be on schedule."

Mack gingerly sat in car. A call came over the radio just as Hew turned the key in the ignition. It was a woman’s voice. Mack listened to the Swiss German conversation not understanding a single word.

Hew handed Mack back his license and said, "I am to drive you to *Kloster Einsiedeln*. That is the large monastery in our town." He shifted the car into gear and pulled out onto the road. He pushed down hard on the accelerator and said, "You must be very important."

"Why do you say that?"

"I have been ordered to drive you to the back entrance of the *Kloster* and make sure you get safely inside. Only important people use the back entrance. Then I am to wait there until I am given new orders."

"I don't understand."

"Neither do I," Hew said.

After an uncomfortable silence, Hew asked, “How did you avoid that accident?”

Mack gently fingered his nose. “I don’t know if it was an accident.”

Hew eased on the accelerator. “Why do you say that?”

Mack explained the BMW bumping from behind as they rounded the curve and the truck coming around the curve in his lane.

“If you find out anything about the drivers, I’d

appreciate a call," Mack said handing Hew his card.

"I don't need that. I know how to get a hold of you."

Hew drove past the twin bell towers of *Kloster Einsiedeln*, the sprawling monastery situated on the west side of town. He followed the road as it curved around the medieval structure. At the back of the monastery, he turned onto the grounds and drove along the stables. Mack looked across the road at the rolling fields and watched a small herd of horses run along the fence line, racing the car. The smell of hay began to permeate the air.

At the far end of the stables, Hew turned right and stopped in front of an iron gate leading into a small paddock. On the wall was a scanner the size of an iPad.

Hew strolled up and placed his hand on the scanner. The gate slid open and Hew turned to Mack. "This is as far as I go." He gestured with his arm for Mack to enter.

"Thank you, Herr Hew."

"Herr Hew is my father. Call me Lucas."

Mack laughed as he shook Hew's hand.

~

Mack stood in front of a metal door as a band of light swept up and down his body. Thirty-seconds later, the metal door slid open. Standing in the doorway was a stunning woman with forest green eyes, shoulder-length blonde hair and aviator-style glasses resting on her celestial nose. She wore an unbuttoned denim shirt over a red Rolling Stones t-shirt. The shirt matched her red lipstick. Her black leggings and ankle boots showed off her shapely legs.

She held out her hand and smiled easily. "William

Alan McMillan, I presume. Or, should I say Billy Mack. I'm Caroline, come in."

Mack took her hand and distractedly shook it. Nimesh was right. She was an exceptional beauty. He was surprised the Rolling Stones were still together.

Caroline took a half step to the right and waved to Hew. "Thank you Lucas, this won't take long."

Mack followed her inside, past a row of offices and into a large circular room. In the middle of the room, five desks stood in a semi-circle facing a large screen bolted to the wall.

On top of each desk was a laptop computer. The laptops were identical, having a heavy metallic, industrial look.

Caroline easily picked up one of the laptops. "This baby weighs just under one pound. It can be bombed, shot with an assault rifle or dropped from an airplane and will still run faster than any computer out there."

"Where can I get one?" Mack asked.

"You can't, but I'm letting you use one until we find Layla. I've already programmed one so you are the only authorized user. All you need to do is apply your thumbprint to the scanner."

"Will someone give me a quick tutorial?"

"The computer will do that when you use it for the first time. She has the most sophisticated artificial intelligence available. She's almost human. I'm giving you Trinity. You'll like her." Caroline said then turned and walked away. As she strolled to the door, she raised her hand over her shoulder and wiggled her fingers for Mack to follow.

"Trinity?" Mack asked as he hurried to catch up.

"That's her name. If you don't call her by her name, she gets prissy and won't talk to you."

"Unbelievable."

"Get used to it."

Caroline led the way into a conference room. Two leather recliners stood in the middle of the room. "Before we start, I need to know if you have any idea why there was an attempt on your life this morning?"

The question took Mack by surprise. "How do you know there was an attempt on my life?"

"I watched the whole thing. The truck moved into the on-coming lane before you rounded the curve. The truck driver had to know you were about to round the curve."

Mack shrugged his shoulders. "You seem to know more than I do."

He considered telling her the man driving the BMW was also following him in Klosters. After a quick deliberation, he decided he would wait and see if she already knew.

"Except the why," Caroline said as she dimmed the lights. "You need to think about that."

Mack knew she was right. It was apparent he had to keep his guard up if he was going to find Layla and get her back home safe and sound.

"Sit down, Billy. The show is about to start."

Mack sat, leaned back and prepared himself for the worst. A grainy nighttime picture of an empty street came to life on to the wall in front of him. It was a video of Main Street in Coconut Grove, south of Miami. The streetlights were in full glow. From the left, two teenage girls walked into the picture as they came under the glow of the streetlight. Mack recognized Layla right away. He couldn't keep a sad smile from invading his lips. He assumed the small blonde girl next to Layla was her friend Holly. They were laughing as they walked. At they approached the street corner, two black SUVs raced up then skidded to a stop as the doors flew open. A large, muscular man lifted Layla off her feet while a second man pulled a black sack down over Layla's head then grabbed her flailing legs. The two men tossed her into the back seat and jumped in after. The sad smile disappeared from Mack's lips.

A short, wiry young man had snuck up behind Holly and swung what looked to be a leather blackjack, hitting her in the back of the head. Her knees buckled and her head went limp. The small man bear-hugged her before she fell then grabbed her breasts with both hands. He carried her ten feet to a dumpster and tossed her inside. He was strong for such a little man. He hurried back to the second SUV. Mack noted the demented smirk on the little man's face as he climbed back into the SUV. He burned that image into his mind.

Mack asked, "Are you able to identify any of those three?"

"Yes, I've identified the man who threw the sack over Layla's head. I'll go over what we know after you watch the entire video."

The video switched to an airport tarmac.

"This is the private charter terminal at Miami International Airport."

A white limousine drove into the picture and stopped near a private jet. Caroline paused the video.

"I'm zooming in so you can get a good look at the faces, if possible."

Mack leaned forward. Two large, muscular men stepped out of the limo and kept their heads turned away from the camera. As soon Layla stepped out of the limo, Mack recognized her. She looked up and slowly turned her head. The camera got a good look at her face.

"Good girl," Mack whispered.

The small, wiry man who'd thrown Holly in the dumpster crawled out of the limo and shoved Layla from behind. She stumbled forward before catching her balance. He kept his head down as he rushed over and grabbed Layla's hand. He pulled her up the steps of the plane and shoved her inside. One of the muscular men followed her into the jet, keeping his face hidden from the camera. The other large man stood guard outside the plane until the door was closed. When the engines roared to life, he strolled away.

"Those two are pros," Caroline said. The little punk abusing Layla is an amateur. That means he's dangerous, unpredictable.

"Does the amateur have a name?"

"We're still running our facial recognition programs. He's young so his age will make him difficult to identify. Trinity has his pictures and she'll be running facial recognition until she can identify him."

"I'm getting to like Trinity."

Caroline laughed and said, "We've identified the one bodyguard who didn't get on the plane. His name is

Hector Rodriquez, a Venezuelan national wanted in a few countries for murder. A year ago, he was arrested in Caracas for fomenting revolution against the Marxist government. After his arrest, he disappeared and hadn't been seen from since, until yesterday."

"How was he able to get into Miami?"

Caroline simply stared at Mack.

"Sorry, my bad. What about the private jet?"

"The plane flew to Barcelona. We lost eyes once it entered a private hanger in Barcelona."

~

CHAPTER 6

The video on the wall faded away and the lights in the room gradually came back to life. Mack pushed himself up out of the leather recliner. "Looks like I'm going to Barcelona," he said.

Caroline vehemently shook her head. "Leave it to the pros. They have the right experience, the right contacts, the language skills, and they know what needs to be done."

"This is personal. I have experience with J Otis Weil and know how that weasel operates. Plus, I have a sense of urgency no one else can match. I can use it to my advantage."

"Billy, J Otis Weil has assembled a team of professionals. You don't know what you're up against."

"I gotta do what I gotta do."

Caroline exhaled in frustration. "That's what Nimesh and Ray Gunn said you'd say so I've reluctantly agreed and have a jet available to take you," she said, not hiding her displeasure. "Hew will drive you to the airfield. A quick word to the wise. Don't panic if it looks like Hew is driving you out to a secluded spot. The airfield doesn't officially exist. It's used exclusively by *Die Uskochte* (Caroline pronounced it *ush-coke-tah).* They are a small, elite special ops team that also doesn't officially exist. *Die Uskochte* roughly means 'your cooked' in Swiss German. They never fail, they just *do. Die Uskochte's* primary mission is to rescue captured, kidnapped or otherwise endangered Swiss citizens living, working or vacationing abroad... among other duties. They don't leave witnesses."

"Never heard of them."

"And you never will. They are the elite of the elite. Your Navy Seal Team Six trains with them once a year. Each Seal Team Six member must sign a strict non-disclosure agreement before even being considered for the training."

Caroline handed Mack a clipboard. "Sign this. It's the aforementioned non-disclosure agreement. No signature no flight."

Mack perused the agreement to find where he was to sign. He grinned and said, "Like I said, I gotta do what I gotta do," then signed the bottom.

There was a knock at the door. A tall woman wearing a blue flight suit stood in the doorway. Her blonde hair was cut into a quasi-Mohawk. Her piercing blue eyes zeroed in on Mack. She looked Mack up and down. "He my cargo?"

Mack picked up on her disparaging tone and grinned.

Caroline nodded and replied, "This is Billy Mack." She gestured to the doorway. "Billy, this is Rikki Ryman, she's the top pilot for *Die Uskochte*. She's also the best pilot in Switzerland, bar none."

Rikki nodded her concurrence. "I'll meet him at the *Missile*," she said and walked away.

Mack gave Caroline a quizzical look. "*Missile*?"

"It's the nickname of the Aerion AS2. It's the world's fastest non-military jet. It's supersonic, flying at Mach 1.6. There are currently only two in operation in the world, one with your CIA and the other with *Die Uskochte*. This machine will get you to Barcelona in twenty minutes, twenty-five if you have to circle the airport before being cleared to land."

"Cool." Mack felt like a child about to walk into Disney World for the first time.

"I still think you should take my advice and let us handle this. Go back to Klosters and do some mountain runs. I'll have a case of *Puntigamer* Beer delivered."

Mack simply shook his head. How the hell did she know he was in Klosters? He shot Caroline a penetrating look and said, "As tempting as the *Puntigamer* offer is, I'm doing this."

"Well, then good luck."

"I don't believe in luck," Mack replied.

"You're the first baseball player I've met who didn't believe in luck or wasn't superstitious."

"Luck is something you make. But I am superstitious, just like every other ballplayer."

Caroline said, "In any case, I have initiated all our eavesdropping and surveillance capabilities across Europe and in Miami. Nimesh and I will stay in constant contact until Layla is home safe and sound. One of us will contact you whenever we have something. You do the same." Caroline adjusted her Aviator glasses. "Time for you to go. Lucas will meet you outside." She handed the industrial laptop computer to Mack. "Take care of Trinity and she'll take care of you."

As they walked to the door, Mack asked, "Is it true you dated both Mick Jagger and Keith Richards?"

"Not Keith, he was married. I went out with Mick once. He's a good guy but I'm more the Enrique Iglesias-type."

Mack half-expected Iglesias to walk into the room.

He finally stuck out his hand. "Thank you Caroline."

"Let me ask you something, Billy. This is important so think about your answer."

Mack nodded.

"Do you think this morning's attempt on your life is connected to Layla's kidnapping and if so, why?"

Mack chewed on his lower lip as he contemplated his reply.

"They are definitely connected," he finally said. "If I can figure out why, I'll find Layla."

~

Outside, Mack found Hew digging through the trunk of a silver Volvo. The Porsche SUV was nowhere in sight.

Hew glanced out of the corner of his eye then

quickly slammed the trunk and strolled to the driver's door. He gestured for Mack to hurry. "Let's go, wheels up in twenty."

"Where's the Porsche?" Mack asked.

"What Porsche?" Hew answered and sat in the driver's seat.

Mack tossed his travel bag in the backseat. He opened the front passenger door and placed Trinity against the front console.

Hew pushed hard on the accelerator and whirled the steering wheel to the left. The Volvo fishtailed around the corner and shot forward. "I love driving fast," Hew said.

They drove in silence for a few minutes until Hew broke the silence. "How do you like Klosters?"

It took Mack a second to realize Caroline must have briefed Hew. "I love it, winter and summer. There's excellent hiking in summer and great skiing in winter. Do you ski?"

Hew grinned. "I'm Swiss. We're born with our skis on."

"Your poor Swiss mothers," Mack replied.

Hew laughed and pushed down on the accelerator.

Mack kept his gaze on the monastery's twin bell towers as they flew by. He said, "I find it interesting that an intelligence service operates out of a monastery."

"If you knew the history of *Kloster Einsiedeln*, or in English, The Einsiedeln Abbey, it would make perfect sense."

"Educate me."

"The Abbey was founded in the ninth century by

Saint Meinrad, a hermit. After robbers killed him, hermits inhabited the Abbey for the next hundred years. Today, the Abbey is dedicated to Our Lady of the Hermits."

"So are you saying the best place to hide an intelligence operation is in a location dedicated to people who don't want to be found?"

"I never thought of that," Hew replied as he softly nodded his head. "It also helps that this particular Abbey is not part of any dioceses or subject to a bishop. The brilliance of an intelligence service operating inside an abbey is that no one would suspect an abbey as a base of operations for anything other than a cloister for monks."

"Gotta love the Swiss."

Hew chuckled and said, "Everybody loves the Swiss. Even those who hate us secretly love us. *Hopp Schwiiz*."

The Volvo slowed as they approached a narrow bridge traversing a large lake. Mack looked across the lake at the snow-capped Alps.

"*Scheisse*, I was afraid of that." Hew said.

~

CHAPTER 7

Mack looked around for anything suspicious while Hew kept his eyes glued to the rearview mirror.

"Why'd you just say *shit*?" Mack asked, swiveling his head left and right.

"We have a tail a hundred meters behind us, a black Peugeot. It's been on us since the monastery." Hew replied.

"How did they know where we were?"

"Someone must have followed us from the scene of the accident."

Hew brought a set of binoculars to his eyes and aimed them down the long bridge cutting low across the lake. "The far side looks clear." He dropped the binoculars to the floorboard, reached to his side and released the snap on his holster. "Just in case," he said to Mack.

"Why are we crossing here?"

"This is the *Sihlsee*, or Lake Sihl. It's not really a lake, it's a reservoir that generates the power we use to run our train system," Hew answered hoping to take Mack's mind off the tail. "We cross this bridge then head north to the airfield. We should be there in ten minutes. Going around the lake would take us an hour to get to our destination."

"Why is the bridge so narrow?" Mack asked, glancing behind him. He saw the black Peugeot idling a hundred meters back.

"I don't know. I didn't build it."

The bridge was immaculate. Mack busied his mind by thinking about the ingenuity and quality he'd seen on his trips to the various parts of Switzerland. Everything worked in this country. The quality of life was tops in the world and the roads, bridges, and tunnels were pristine, no potholes, bumps or even blemishes. The public transport was top quality and ran on time. Mack looked at his Swiss watch, a reliable silver *Tag Heuer*. Mack wanted the rest of his trip to run like his Swiss watch: reliable and steady.

Hew crept the Volvo onto the bridge then cautiously increased his speed. He kept the Volvo at a steady pace as they crossed the bridge.

When they reached the other side of the lake, Mack blew a sigh of relief.

Hew pressed down on the accelerator while his eyes constantly checked the rearview mirror. As they rounded the corner, Hew slammed on the brakes and the Volvo skidded to a stop. A white Ford utility van was tipped onto its side and resting in the middle of the road. The van partially blocked both lanes and smoke billowed from the engine.

A young woman with long black hair stood next to the van holding her hands up as if in prayer then gestured desperately for help. She wore a jean jacket over a yellow sundress. There were blotches of blood on the dress.

Mack fixated on the van as the smell of burning rubber infiltrated the car. A shadow through the van's windshield caught his eye. He spied a pair of boots creeping along the far side of the gray van.

"This is a set-up, Lucas. There's someone on the other side of the van crouched and moving steadily toward us."

Hew cautiously stepped out with his hand gripping his sidearm, a camouflaged Sphinx 3000 - standard issue. "Is everything okay?" he asked the woman in Swiss German.

"Please help me," the woman replied in English.

A short, burly man with unkempt, greasy hair leapt from behind the van with his pistol in the firing position and pulled the trigger.

Mack saw the bullet rip through Hew's left bicep. Hew twirled and fell to the ground. He raised his pistol as he rolled onto his back and aimed it at the young woman. He fired before he sat up.

The bullet was a perfect kill shot, hitting her in the chest and exploding her heart. She fell straight backward, hitting the asphalt then bouncing up a few inches. A machine pistol fell from underneath her jean jacket and landed on the road next to her.

The burly man turned his attention to Mack and aimed.

Mack lifted Trinity in front of his chest to act as a bulletproof vest. The man fired and Mack felt the impact of the bullet hitting Trinity's metal casing before he saw the bullet hole pierce the windshield. The bullet ricocheted into the dashboard.

The short, stocky man took a step toward the car then turned his attention to Hew lying on the ground. A rabid smile sullied his face. He glanced over at Mack and his eyes widened. "Don't go anywhere Billy Mack, I'll be back for you."

He started toward Hew.

Mack stepped out of the Volvo to distract the crazed man. "Why make me wait? Come at me first?"

"I've been ordered to bring you with me so shut the fuck up." He turned his attention back to Hew and marched toward him.

Hew sat up like he was doing a sit-up and fired, hitting the gunman in the groin.

The greasy man dropped his pistol, grunted as he bent over, and grabbed his crotch.

"You shoot a man in his bratwurst and his hunger for a fight is gone," Hew said.

The burly man lifted his eyes, stared at Hew with his rabid smile slowly returning. He reached for his pistol.

Before Mack could move, Hew raised his pistol again and shot the man through the top of his greasy head. He held his pistol up until the man crumpled face-first to the asphalt.

Hew blew on the end of the barrel. "Just like Bruce Willis in Die Hard."

Mack ran to the Volvo and popped the trunk. He rifled through a crate filled with guns, surveillance equipment and protective gear until he found a first-aid kit.

He hurried over to Hew, poured a bottle of sterile saline solution on the bullet hole in Hew's left bicep then packed gauze over the wound and taped an X around his arm.

"We need to hurry. We may have more visitors soon," Mack said.

Hew stood, wobbled a bit then caught his balance. With his foot, he rolled the dead man over and clicked a picture of his face. He strolled over to the young woman and clicked another picture. "I'm sending these to Caroline for identification."

"What do we do with the bodies?" Mack asked.

"Leave them here to rot." Hew studied the screen on his phone. "Good. Caroline's been busy. The road is being blocked from both directions. A chopper will be here soon to take the bodies away. A tow truck is on its way to take the van to our lab. If we leave now, we'll be through the roadblock before those tailing us can catch up."

In the distance, Mack saw a helicopter approaching. "How could they already know?"

Hew raised his eyebrows telling Mack he wouldn't be answering that question. Instead, he said, "Let's go, you have a plane to catch."

Knowing he shouldn't ask any follow-up questions,

Mack said. "You need medical attention. Let me drive you to the hospital."

"There's a field hospital next to the airport. Better I go there so I don't have to answer any questions," Hew replied as he carefully lowered himself backward into the driver's seat and swiveled forward. "Get in or we'll be late."

Hew crept the Volvo around the van then sped down the road at top speed. Mack eyed the helicopter closing fast. Snow-capped mountain peaks hovered in the background. The mountains looked close but Mack knew the peaks were at least a thirty-minute drive away — or fifteen minutes the way Hew was driving. He clutched Trinity to his chest and fingered the dent from the bullet.

Hew turned onto a one-lane road running along the lakeshore. The asphalt was painted green, matching the color of the field it ran through.

Up ahead, Mack caught the glimmer of the sun reflecting off something metallic at the base of a green and gray mountain. Mack squinted hoping to make out the object.

"That's the airfield up ahead," Hew explained. "The farmhouse over there on the right is the field hospital."

Mack squinted again but couldn't see the airfield.

Hew drove the Volvo into a tunnel and slowed to a stop. Forty meters ahead was a sleek train car. A loud noise sounding like an engine being revved echoed down the mountain tunnel. Rikki Ryman stood inside the train car with her hands on her hips.

The gauze covering the bullet hole in Hew's left bicep was soaked in blood and seeping down his shirt. He stuck out his right hand. "Good luck Billy."

Mack shook Hew's hand. "Thank you, Lucas. Get yourself to the field hospital." He slid Trinity under his arm, snatched his overnight bag from the back seat then climbed out of the car and shut the door. He peeked over at Rikki standing inside the train car then bent down and leaned in through the Volvo's open window. "You're not a cop, are you, Lucas." It wasn't a question.

Hew grinned, and with a wink, said, "Let's say I like to cook."

"I owe you big, real big," Mack yelled over the engine noise as he marched to the train car.

Hew shouted, "My wife and I will ski with you in Klosters this season, your treat."

Walking away, Mack waved his hand over his shoulder. He shouted back, "You're on. See you there."

~

Mack climbed into the sleek train car and nodded hello to Rikki.

Rikki pointed at a seat. "Sit down and buckle up."

She sat in the facing seat and buckled her seat belt.

As soon as Mack buckled up, the train shot forward, the force pushing Mack hard against his seat back.

Mack tried to act nonchalant but was not doing a very good job. Rikki grinned at him as she sat comfortably in her seat. Mack wondered what she was thinking.

"Relax Mr. McMillan. Don't fight it."

Mack grinned back at her. "Mr. McMillan is my father. Call me Billy."

"We'll be at our destination shortly, Mr. McMillan."

The train slowed and came to a stop near a long, sleek private jet with the nose section bend downward. It was a smaller version of the Concorde.

The train doors slid open automatically and Rikki jumped out. Mack unbuckled his seatbelt and hurried to catch up.

"Where's the runway?" Mack asked.

"We're walking on it," Rikki replied with an impish grin.

Mack only saw the rounded walls of the tunnel lit by halogen lights. There was no natural light coming from either direction.

"Help me out," Mack said. "I don't see a runway."

"You worry too much, Mr. McMillan. Get in the plane and let me do what I do best."

Mack climbed the stairs of the plane, followed by Rikki.

"There's a compartment for your bags in the back," Rikki said. She walked to the cockpit and closed the door with a bang.

Mack dropped his bag into the compartment and brought Trinity with him to his seat.

"Fasten your seatbelt Mr. McMillan," Rikki said over the intercom. "We're departing now. As soon as we're airborne, you can use your devices. There is also a wet bar above the compartment where you stored your bag. We have your precious *Puntigamer* beer, how you like it, in cans."

Mack stared out the window into the blackness as

the plane eased ahead then suddenly shot forward. Mack closed his eyes and prayed as the plane began to rattle.

When he felt the plane lift off the ground, he opened his eyes. The plane soared out of the tunnel and into blue sky. Mack looked back to see only the sheer face of a mountain. High up in the rock face was an opening where the runway ended. He eased his grip on the armrest.

The plane rose sharply, increasing its speed. Off in the distance, Mack saw the Mediterranean Sea.

As his composure returned, Mack checked his phone to see two missed calls from Nimesh and one from Ray Gunn.

He called Nimesh to learn that Hector Rodriquez, one of Layla's kidnappers, the man who did not get on the plane in Miami, was found shot to death execution style in Little Havana. Nimesh was checking with his contacts to determine his killer. Initial intelligence pointed to an assassin tied to the Russian government.

Nimesh had sent a photo of the small, wiry kidnapper to a contact at the NSA. They were running all their recognitions programs but so far had very little. One program identified the young man's facial features as Basque but hadn't matched his photos with known Basque criminals, separatists or anyone with a record.

Before Mack called Gunn, he placed Trinity on the table in front of him, lifted the screen and placed his thumb on the fingerprint reader. The screen immediately came to life with a satellite photo of Barcelona.

A voice emanated from the speakers. "Hello Billy Mack. I am Trinity. Nice to meet you. I have been running recognition programs to determine who abducted Layla but so far have nothing to report. I have a message from Caroline. She has sent us the address in Barcelona of the safe house we are to use while we are there. A driver will meet us when we land and take us there. That is all I have for you right now."

Mack closed the screen and called Gunn.

"Hello Cece, it's Billy. Is Ray available?"

"Hi Billy. I am sorry about your niece. Everyone here is praying for her and you. Ray has been waiting for your call."

She put the call through.

"Billy, how are you holding up?" Gunn asked.

Mack didn't feel the need to say how he was coping. "Any news?" he asked.

"Your sister just received a ransom call. Kessler was there when the call came in."

As he waited for his boss to continue, Mack listened to Gunn softly clicking his tongue against the roof of his mouth.

Gunn finally said, "I don't understand the ransom demand. It's very strange and doesn't sound good, no matter how you slice it."

"What do you mean?"

"Let me play the call for you."

~

CHAPTER 8

J Otis Weil's limousine pulled to a stop in front of a dilapidated, four-story apartment building in the *El Raval* neighborhood of Barcelona. *El Raval*, once known as Barcelona's Chinatown, bordered the port of Barcelona and was infamous for its poverty, prostitution and crime.

The limousine parked two wheels on the curb so as not to block traffic. The narrow street was dotted with dented cargo vans parked haphazardly. A dreary gray cloudbank was rolling in from the Mediterranean, casting a pall over the city.

The street level windows of the tired, old apartment building were boarded up and each board was tagged with the same gang symbol.

Under normal circumstances, J Otis would never

consider coming into a slum like this. If something were needed from such a place, he would send one of his expendable minions. But in this case, Layla was here. He would crawl through a mile of broken glass and tacks to be with her — or force one of his minions to crawl for him. But, he would feel their pain.

J Otis pressed the button next to his seat lowering the window separating the chauffeur from the passenger seats. "Go ring apartment number five and have someone come down and meet me at the door," J Otis said from the back seat. He raised the divider before the chauffeur could reply.

The chauffeur jumped out and hurried to the front door. He pressed the buzzer and repeated J Otis's instructions.

When the lobby door opened, J Otis recognized Jordi, Nuria's son. Jordi scared the bejesus out of him. The boy wasn't right. You could see it in his eyes.

J Otis strutted his diminutive frame down the sidewalk to the door. The last thing he would do was display any fear or apprehension in front of Jordi. J Otis was the boss and Jordi needed constant reminding.

J Otis nodded confidently to Jordi and said, "Lead the way." He stayed three steps behind Jordi, close enough not to show fear. On the third floor landing, J Otis knocked once on the door and pushed it open.

Nuria stood across the room, bent over with her right hand pressed against the wall. She was deep in the throws of a coughing fit. In her left hand was a lit cigarette.

"Great," J Otis murmured. Walking toward her, he

grinned and said, "You don't sound good. Are you going to make it? Don't die until I get my money."

"Fuck you too, J Otis. I'll be around until I get what I deserve... and you get what you deserve." Nuria pointed to the kitchen. "Let's go in there."

She strolled over to her son, kissed him on the lips and said, "Keep an eye on the door, my baby."

J Otis followed her into a dingy kitchen. The shoddy appliances were fifty years old and spotted with rust. The floor was bare concrete. Black grease streaks ran down the walls.

Nuria pulled her bottle of *DYC Whisky* from the cabinet and snatched a dirty glass from the sink. She turned the glass upside down, shook out a wet cigarette butt and poured the glass half full with whiskey. She gulped down a large swallow then exhaled slowly until her throat quit burning.

She held the bottle up. "Want a swig, partner?"

J Otis didn't like the way she said *partner*. She was mocking him but he let it pass. The sooner he was out of this shithole, the better. He held up his hand and said, "No, I don't have time. Did your *other pro* get Mack?" J Otis pronounced *'other pro'* with disdain.

"I haven't heard from her yet."

"Then we assume she failed and we go to plan B. I'll go up and get the girl. When I get back down, we make the call."

"Jordi," Nuria yelled. "Go get-"

J Otis cut her off, "That little *misfit* is not going anywhere near her until this is over. That's what we agreed." J Otis glared at Nuria. He knew showing even the slightest sign of weakness was risky. "I'll go get her."

"No you won't. Not until I get my justice. When we make the call, I'll order Nacho to bring her to us."

Nuria refilled her glass and marched out of the kitchen without uttering a word. She sat in the living room and waited for J Otis.

J Otis strolled out of the kitchen and eyed Jordi. He repositioned a chair so he faced both Nuria and Jordi. It was self-preservation. He didn't like having his back to either one.

"When we make the call, you do the talking," J Otis said. "Remember to stick to the script." J Otis glanced over at Jordi then said in a low voice, "Billy Mack brings the three million dollars from Layla's trust in non-sequential hundred dollar bills split evenly in two Adidas duffel bags to Barcelona. When he arrives in Barcelona, he will receive detailed instructions of where to deliver the money."

Nuria shook her head. "Billy Mack carries one bag and the killer carries the other. It has to be that way or I kill the girl."

"Fine, get Layla down here and make the call."

Nuria walked to the base of the stairs. She cleared her throat and yelled, "Nacho, bring the girl down." As soon as she finished, she flew into another coughing fit, making no attempt to cover her mouth. When the fit subsided, Nuria lit a cigarette to calm her nerves.

Layla came down the steps in her bra and panties. Nacho had his left arm wrapped around her neck and his right hand over her mouth.

At the bottom of the steps, Jordi hurried over and

took Layla from Nacho. He put his left arm around her back, pulled her close then clamped his hand over her left breast. A wide smile stretched across his lips as he clamped his right hand over Layla's mouth and squeezed harder than needed.

Layla showed no emotion, no fear.

Nacho walked out of the room.

J Otis let Jordi have his thrill. The last thing he needed right now was to upset the unstable psycho.

Nuria held the satellite phone in front of her face, punched in the number then brought the phone to her ear and waited.

J Otis heard the click of the connection and cocked his ear.

"Hel... Hello," a woman's voice stammered.

Nuria exhaled a cloud of smoke then said, "If you want to see Layla again, here is what you do. Take the three million dollars deposited in Layla's trust and place the money evenly in two identical Adidas duffel bags. Make sure the money is in non-sequential, hundred dollar bills. Have the money in Barcelona by tomorrow afternoon. Billy Mack and John Kessler must be here to deliver the bags, together. When I confirm they are in Barcelona, Billy Mack will receive a call with detailed delivery instructions."

Nuria heard muffled voices on the other end of the connection.

"I need proof Layla is unharmed. Let me talk to her."

Nuria motioned for Jordi to bring Layla to the phone.

Nuria glared at Layla as she held her hand over the

mouthpiece. She said, "You say what you were instructed and nothing more." She raised her hand threatening to slap Layla.

Layla tried to lift her chin up.

When Jordi removed his hand, Layla said, "Mom, Dad, Billy, I'm okay. I'm being treated fine. Better than the dead cop in Penzance."

Jordi slapped Layla hard then quickly clamped his hand back over her mouth. His left hand began massaging her left breast.

Nuria marched over and whispered in Layla's ear, "You little bitch. You will pay for that." She brought the phone back to her ear.

"If there is a problem getting the ransom money how do we contact you?"

Nuria stared at the phone. She didn't expect to hear a man's voice. "Who the fuck is speaking?"

"The person who is going to kill you if you lay a hand on Layla."

"Just bring the fucking money, asshole. You have until tomorrow afternoon," Nuria said as she jammed her finger down hard on the power button.

"Who the fuck was that?" she mumbled.

J Otis simply shrugged his shoulders. He said, "I'm taking Layla back upstairs."

"No, you're not," Nuria answered then yelled out, "Nacho, take the little bitch upstairs."

"Fine," J Otis replied, "then you and I leave right now to secure the new location."

~

CHAPTER 9

In Coral Gables, Kessler hung up the phone, flicked off the digital recorder and turned to Terri and Hermi.

"The only good thing is-"

Terri cut him off, "Why are the kidnappers requiring *you and Billy* to deliver the ransom?"

Kessler frowned as he shrugged his shoulders. "I know as much as you do right now. I'll make a few calls and let you know what I learn." Kessler waited for a response that never came then walked to the front door. "If they call back, make sure the recorder is working."

Sitting in his car, Kessler wracked his brain to figure out why he and Mack were ordered to deliver the ransom money together. He understood having Billy Mack deliver the money but why was he involved.

He called Ray Gunn in Chicago. "It's me," Kessler said. "The call we expected just ended. It was unusual. The kidnappers demanded three million in cash, not unexpected. But, the rest of the instructions came out of left field. The money is to come from Layla's trust account. How did they know about that? Also, and this is the most puzzling part. One of the kidnappers is a woman and she demanded Mack and I deliver the money. Why am I in the middle?"

"*Hmmm.* Why do you think?" Gunn asked. "Did you identify yourself on the phone?"

"No, but I did lay down the law and threaten to kill anyone involved if Layla was harmed in any way. I never gave my name. Only a handful of people know I'm involved."

"Time to think outside the box," Gunn replied. "While we think, I'll have the three million within the hour then fly it down to Miami. I will arrange for an Aerion AS2 to come pick you up and fly you to Barcelona. It's supersonic so your flight will only take three hours. Be ready to leave by five this afternoon."

"Get me diplomatic clearance. I'm bringing my power tools."

"It's already done. I also called Mack's uncle, Cardinal Kauftheil. Mack already spoke to him. The Cardinal has arranged for our mutual friend to meet you in Barcelona. She's on her way."

"You think that's wise?"

"She knows the landscape."

"That's not what I'm talking about."

"I know, but you're both professionals, the best in

the business and are needed now. You two need to put the past behind you until Layla is safe and sound."

"Easier said than done."

~

Rikki landed the *Missile* at El Prat Airport outside Barcelona so softly Mack thought the runway was a sponge. The flight time was so short Mack only had time to listen to the ransom call recording once.

He stared out the window as the plane rolled to a stop near a nondescript hanger. A black Chevy Suburban was parked next to the hanger door. The windows on the SUV were as dark as its glossy paint job.

The cockpit door opened and Rikki strolled over to Mack. "How was your flight, Mr. McMillan?"

"Too fast."

"I wasn't even flying at full speed." She shot Mack a cocky grin.

She lowered the steps and gestured for Mack to de-plane. "I've been instructed to pick up Mr. Kessler and deliver him here."

Rikki followed Mack to the Suburban, gave instructions in Catalan to the driver then turned to Mack. "It will take you longer to drive to the house than the flight took from Switzerland. Since I've been ordered to Miami to pick up your partner, I will be gone for six or seven hours."

Mack waited for Rikki to board the plane then he turned and climbed into the Suburban and sat back.

Mack's phone vibrated then rang. He fished it out of his pocket. It was Caroline.

"I have two pieces of information for you, Billy."

"Before you begin," Mack replied, "can I assume no one knows I'm here so I shouldn't expect any surprises on the drive into Barcelona like I had in Switzerland?"

"There are no guarantees in life, Billy. But, you're in a bombproof, steel-plated vehicle with bulletproof glass. It would take a bunker-buster bomb to take you out."

"That's not what I asked."

"As far as I know, only Rikki, Lucas and I know you're there. If you've told someone, that's on you."

Caroline waited to see if Mack had more questions.

She finally said, "I have two pieces of information for you. First, as you heard, the ransom call was made. I've sent the recording to Trinity for analysis."

"Why did the woman demand John Kessler be part of the ransom drop?" Mack asked.

"Good question. I ran a few programs to determine where there is a connection between Kessler, Oriol Consultaria, JOW Holdings, you and Penzance."

"I rescued Layla when she was held captive in Penzance by a dirty, pedophile cop. That cop is dead."

"I know, but every program I ran came up blank. I'm expanding the parameters now."

"Check for any dead cops from Barcelona or *Cataluña*."

"I ran that algorithm and nothing came up."

"Layla was giving us a clue." Mack said firmly.

"I'll keep expanding my search," Caroline said.

"What else do you have?"

"One of our eavesdropping programs picked up a call this morning between Zurich and Barcelona when some of my key words was flagged. Those key words were 'Billy Mack.'"

Mack was not surprised. There was one attempt on his life and one attempt to abduct him in Switzerland. He became concerned that the kidnappers would already know the two teams in Switzerland had failed. He thought of the repercussions for Layla.

"Is that all?" Mack asked.

"We have the identity of one of the callers and maybe the name of the person on the other end of the call. The phone with the Swiss number and is registered to JOW Holdings and Sunden Capital. I ran a voice recognition program and identified the voice on that phone as J Otis Weil, a man you're familiar with. He thinks his phone is secure." Caroline chuckled. "Sunden Capital is based in Moscow but has an office in Zürich. The other phone is registered to *Oriol Consultoria*, a Barcelona company owned jointly by Nuria Oriol and JOW Holdings. The company's Barcelona office has an address in *Cuitat Vella*... that means 'old city' in Catalan. The company address turns out to be just a post office box. I can't run voice recognition on the woman because I have no one to compare it to."

"Is the safe house near *Cuitat Vella*?" Mack asked.

"Sorry, no, the safe house is in the *Sarria* neighborhood in the northwest part of the city. The street is *Carrer del Milanesat*. From there, you have excellent access to the entire city."

"How far is the house from *Cuitat Vella*?"

"You're roughly ten minutes northwest of there as the crow flies," Caroline replied. Before Mack could ask another question, she said, "John Kessler will arrive in six to seven hours with the money in two bags and in the denominations the kidnappers demanded. He will meet you at the safe house."

"Is there anything else I should know?"

"You're up to speed except for one last thing. Ray Gunn asked me to pass a message on to you. This is a direct quote: 'Stay in the safe house until Kessler arrives.'"

"Thank you, Caroline," Mack said and ended the call. He had no intention of staying in the safe house waiting for Kessler.

As the Chevy Suburban raced toward the city, Mack thought of Layla's words: *'Better than the dead cop in Penzance.'* Why would she say that? Knowing Layla like he did, she had a specific reason, a purpose.

The ringing of his cell phone shattered Mack's concentration. The screen read: UNKNOWN. He brought the phone to his ear. He heard a woman's voice.

"Billy Mack, don't say a word, just listen."

~

CHAPTER 10

Mack pressed the phone hard against his ear while his head swiveled back and forth between the front and back windows studying the Barcelona streets. The last two times he was in a car it didn't go well.

Not sensing imminent danger, he returned his attention to the caller, Maite Garcia.

She said, "I've done a preliminary investigation and you have a problem. There's a dirty cop inside *Guàrdia Urbana*, the municipal police force for Barcelona. One of the *Guàrdia's* young officers has been discreetly inquiring about you and Kessler."

"Someone inside the police force knows I'm here?"

"Either that or they're expecting you. I have the officer's name and will pay him a visit when he gets home for lunch today."

"What if he doesn't go home for lunch?"

There was a deep-throated laugh before Garcia said, "In *Cataluña*, most folks, especially cops, don't make much money so they go home for lunch. That means e*very* cop, if he gets off-duty, goes home for lunch. I've confirmed our man is off-duty today."

"Then I'm going with you."

"No, you're not. You're staying in the safe house until Kessler arrives and you get the ransom instructions."

"I can't do that," Mack said.

"Leave this to the pros. We've done this before."

Mack knew she was right but every fiber in his being told him he knew how Layla thought, how she acted when her life was at risk and how she reacted when things went sideways. No one else did.

"Billy, are you still there?" Garcia asked.

"Of course."

"We will get Layla back, I promise. In the meantime, your uncle will be calling you. He's going to make you promise to stay inside the safe house until Kessler arrives. You can't lie to a Cardinal of the Catholic Church and, more importantly, to your uncle, your own blood. Remember, Kessler's a professional. He's the best and knows what to do and what to expect."

Mack knew it was futile to engage in an argument he couldn't win. "Fine, when my uncle calls, I'll promise him I won't leave."

Mack decided not to take his uncle's call until after Kessler arrived with the money.

"Now you're talking sense. We all have one goal, get

Layla back safe and sound. As soon as I extract what I need from the cop, you'll hear from me."

The Chevy Suburban pulled to a stop in front of a Gothic style house. The sandstone bricks on the ground floor were recently sandblasted and the pale yellow paint on the top two floors was fresh. Every window had thick metal bars bolted over the glass. The steel front door was designed to look like wood but had no door handle. Instead, there was an intricate number pad built into the brown steel where the door handle normally was. A small gold sign on the wall next to the door read: N*úmero Cinco S.L.*

Mack grabbed Trinity and his overnight bag. He strolled to the door looking over his shoulder. The driver stood next to the Suburban with a stern look on his face.

As he approached the doorway, the metal door clicked and popped open.

In the doorway stood an athletic man, five-foot ten with shoulder-length shaggy hair, a long face and resolute eyes.

Mack slid Trinity under his left arm and stuck out his right hand. "I'm Billy Mack."

"I'm Carles Puyol. Welcome to Barcelona, Billy." He shook Mack's hand with a firm grip.

"How did you know I was here?" Mack asked.

Puyol held up his phone to show Mack the screen. "Caroline informed me that you were outside. Come in."

Mack walked past Puyol into a large foyer, dropped his overnight bag on the stone floor and laid Trinity on top of the bag. He turned and studied Puyol's face.

"Have we met before?"

Puyol grinned. "I do not believe so."

Mack's eyes widened. "Wait, you're *Carles Puyol*, the footballer."

"No longer," Puyol replied then smiled at what he said. "Well, I'm still Carles Puyol but no longer a footballer. I retired three years ago."

"You were arguably the best defender to play the game, certainly the most commanding. I loved watching you play."

Puyol lowered his eyes as he answered, "Thank you, that is nice of you to say, especially coming from a professional athlete. I understand you were a great baseball player. That is a sport I do not understand. You must tell me about it while we wait for our guests."

"I would enjoy that. In the meantime, where can I put my bags? I want to take a walk and stretch my legs."

"It is my understanding you are instructed to stay inside the house until your American colleague arrives."

Mack wandered around the foyer admiring the modern art on the walls. He recalled the time the White Sox were rumored to be trading him to the Cubs. Mack wanted to stay because the White Sox were on the verge of making the playoffs and back then the Cubs were, well, the Cubs. Against the advice of his agent, Mack went to the Cubs and explained why he wanted to stay with the Sox. During that tense time, Mack read an article about Puyol when he was coming into his own as a soccer player.

"If I remember right, Barcelona wanted to send you to Malaga. Just like me, you refused to go, correct?"

Puyol shrugged. "I don't understand the comparison."

"Against all advice, you listened to your gut because you knew you were right. That was the smartest move you made in your career and look how it turned out for you."

Puyol nodded again. "I know you are here because someone you love is in grave danger. My situation was different. I refused to go to Malaga because I'm Catalan and I knew my career should be in Barcelona. Besides, it was not life and death and I was only person affected."

"You did what you had to do." Mack said, then he explained his history and relationship with Layla. "What's more, nobody knows where I am so it should be safe to meander around and I think better when I walk."

Reading Mack's face, Puyol recalled what Caroline told him about Layla's harsh life in the London sex trade.

Finally, he begrudgingly agreed. "The kidnappers know you're here so I will accompany you. While we walk, I can show you around and tell you what you need to know about Barcelona and *Cataluña*."

"I think better when I'm alone."

"It's not negotiable."

~

CHAPTER 11

Mack stepped out onto the sidewalk and squinted into the late afternoon sun. The clouds had cleared and except for a few wisps of high clouds floating overhead, the sky was white blue.

A shrill voice followed by a thunderclap of applause came from a blaring television in the apartment across the street. Mack caught a glimpse of the small black and white screen before the curtains were pulled closed.

Puyol followed Mack out the front door then he tapped the screen on his phone. The steel door closed with a hiss then a loud click.

Puyol pointed down the street and started walking. He kept pointing as if Mack needed the reminder. If Mack was going anywhere, Puyol was determined to lead him there.

The street veered around a small plaza with two palm trees on a mound in the center. The far side of the plaza abutted a busy road with traffic bumper to bumper.

"That street is *Via Augusta*," Puyol said, nodding toward the heavy traffic. "If you go to the right, down the road, you end up in the city center and the sea. If you go left, up the road, you run into *Tibidabo*, the mountain hovering over the city."

Mack looked up at the green and brown mountain then down the busy street. "I take it *Cuitat Vella* is down the street. How far is it?"

"Yes, the old city is down this way. It will take you thirty minutes to walk there and fifteen minutes to drive. The subway also goes there and takes ten minutes."

Mack walked down the street keeping a vigilant eye on the cars passing by.

Puyol hustled after him and calmly gripped Mack's elbow, stopping him. "Before you go anywhere, let's have a cup of coffee so I can tell you a few things about Barcelona and the Catalans. Things you need to know."

Mack thought about jerking his arm free and continuing his march to the old city then realized he would be stupid to piss off Puyol. He may be useful and insider knowledge in any situation is invaluable.

"Lead the way."

Puyol led Mack away from *Via Augusta.* They

walked down one block then turned right. At the next intersection, a small, posh restaurant was located on the opposite corner. The lunch rush was over and the restaurant was empty. A waitress stood in the doorway watching Puyol and Mack approach. She wore tight black jeans, black heels, a crisp men's white-collar dress shirt and no bra.

"Carles Puyol," she said, her eyes dancing with delight. "Will you be having a late lunch with us? I certainly hope so."

Puyol read her nametag and replied, "No, thank you, Rocio. Just coffee for us today."

Puyol sat at a table in the rear with his back against the wall. He had a direct line of sight to the front door as well as to both streets through the windows.

Mack sat across from him, his back to the door. He was uncomfortable and squirmed in his seat until Puyol said, "Relax, I have your back."

The waitress brought a double espresso and an Americano coffee. She bent over the table and placed the espresso in front of Puyol. "Yours is on the house, Carles," she said.

She put the Americano next to Mack, spilling coffee out onto the saucer. Mack noticed she had unbuttoned the top two buttons on her shirt.

"Tell me what I should know about the Catalans and Barcelona," Mack said after the waitress sashayed away.

"First, you must always remember, we are Catalan first, Spanish second. Some Catalans won't even admit being a part of Spain. The distrust of Madrid runs deep in many. Second, Catalans prefer to deal with other Catalans because they trust them. Outsiders, anyone not Catalan, are not trusted."

Mack thought about Puyol's words. He had heard that most Catalans consider *Cataluña* a separate country. "So, people from say, Andalusia, or Galicia or the Basque Country are considered outsiders?"

Puyol nodded. "They are slightly less despised than the Castilians from Madrid, The *Castellanos*."

"I'll make sure no one thinks I'm from Madrid."

Puyol sipped his coffee.

"What should I know about Barcelona?" Mack asked.

"Barcelona is the capital of *Cataluña*," Puyol replied. He smiled slyly and took another sip of his espresso.

Mack wiped the bottom of his coffee cup with his napkin and brought the cup to his lips. As he drank, he noticed Puyol stand and step away from the table.

Mack placed his cup back onto the wet saucer and cautiously turned around to see Puyol hugging as dark-haired woman wearing an olive tank top, black leather pants and camouflage combat boots. She had a wide smile on her face.

Mack recognized Maite Garcia and stood.

Garcia turned to Mack. "Your uncle, Cardinal Kauftheil can be very persuasive."

"He promised me he would call you," Mack replied.

Her smile was replaced by a scornful glare. "You, on the other hand, promised to stay put until you spoke with the Cardinal." She shook her head in disappointment.

Mack could only grin. He was thankful she was here and shifted the conversation to finding Layla.

"Thank you for coming so quickly," Mack said. "I don't think we have much time."

Her eyes softened. "Ray Gunn reminded me that you don't obey orders well. I usually respect that in a person but in this case, you better have a damn good reason for leaving the safe house."

Garcia waited for Puyol to sit back down and she sat next to him, facing the door. She motioned for Mack to sit.

Her fingers strummed the table waiting for Mack to answer. Cutting through the silence, she finally said, "Billy, give me a good reason."

Mack felt like his sixth grade teacher, Sister Mary Martin, was scolding him.

He sipped his coffee and recalled his explanation to Caroline after she ordered him to leave the search for Layla to the professionals. He said, "I know how Layla thinks, how she acts when her life is at risk and, more importantly, how she reacts when things go sideways. No one else knows her as well as I do."

"Fair enough," Garcia said then glanced momentarily at Puyol. "However, Carles and I have dealt with kidnappers many times. It is more important to know how *they* think."

"I can't argue with that," Mack replied and grinned nervously. "Let's work together, combine our skills, our expertise, as they say?"

Garcia and Puyol caught eyes. It looked to Mack like they were communicating telepathically.

"If we do," Garcia said, "I'm in charge."

"That part's not negotiable," Puyol added.

Mack tensed and ran his hands through his hair.

Before Mack had a chance to respond, Garcia said, "Tell us about Layla."

Her tacit agreement was music to Mack's ears. He said, "Don't be fooled by Layla's size. She as strong as the situation dictates. She's a fighter and she never gives up or gives in. She is very intelligent and her street smarts are off the charts. She's a sweet girl who had a hard life after her father died." Mack explained her life inside the London brothel until she escaped and came into his life.

"That's helpful but dealing with kidnappers is different than dealing with pimps. What do you Americans say? *It's a whole new ballgame.*" Garcia reached over, took a sip of Puyol's espresso and gently set it back down. "When you're dealing with kidnappers, assume the worst."

Mack bit his lip. He couldn't respond to Garcia's statement without getting emotional.

"What can you tell us regarding Layla's kidnapping?" Puyol asked.

Mack sucked in a breath and fought back a tear. He summarized his call with his sister and what Caroline and Nimesh discovered. He ended the summation saying, "On the ransom call Layla said, 'better than the dead cop in Penzance' and that has a specific meaning. That's how Layla operates. She's sending me a message, a clue."

"In Penzance, Layla was held captive by a

pedophile cop, right? Was it for sex?" Garcia asked.

Garcia had done her homework. "Yes, but that pervert was convinced he was in love with Layla and if he kept her long enough, she would eventually love him back."

"Do you know what she meant with that clue?"

"It has something to do with cops, be it a location like a police station or a jail, or something like a police car or a certain cop or detective."

The waitress came by, smiled at Puyol before asking Garcia if she wanted to order.

Garcia waved her away then took another sip of Puyol's espresso.

The waitress shot Garcia the evil eye.

Mack asked, "Did you pay a visit to the cop who was asking questions about Kessler and me?"

Garcia's jaw tightened as she nodded her head with trepidation, or maybe it was dismay. She looked past the front door into the street and held her gaze.

Puyol raised his hands above the table signaling for Mack to sit tight, not say anything.

Garcia returned her gaze to Mack. She exhaled in frustration and said, "I did. It didn't go well."

~

CHAPTER 12

J Otis deftly poured vodka into a glass then sat back and gazed out the window while his limousine cruised down the wide boulevard. He stared up at *Montjuic*, the broad hill overlooking the old city and the Mediterranean Sea. He deliberately ignored Nuria sitting to his right.

Nuria stared out the opposite window. She was uncomfortable being alone with J Otis inside his world of chauffeured limos, five-star hotels and seven-course meals. As the limo circled a four-lane roundabout, she drifted off and thought about her father.

~

Nuria grew up dirt poor in Bilbao, a port city in northwest Spain and the largest city in the Basque

Country. When she was young, her father bitterly opposed Spanish dictator, Francisco Franco, making it impossible for him to find work. Franco and his Nationalist Party made life hell for anyone who openly opposed them. Nuria's father begged, borrowed and stole to feed his family until he couldn't take it any longer. When Nuria was six, her father decided to take matters into his own hands, stole an army uniform and old rifle from a neighbor and headed to city hall with the intention of assassinating *Generalísimo* Francisco Franco. His plan was to walk up and shoot Franco during an official visit to Bilbao. Simple.

His plan nearly worked. The crowd stared in stunned silence at the audacity of a man in uniform marching up to Franco. There was a collective gasp when Nuria's father raised and aimed his rifle at Franco. Unfortunately for Nuria's father, the rifle backfired. He was never seen or heard from again.

~

"Are you sure this place fits our needs?" J Otis asked, disrupting Nuria's recurring nightmare.

"Of course," Nuria replied and shook her head, irritated by J Otis' lack of trust. "The house is big enough, there is a private garage and it is on a quiet street. Upstairs there is a solitary room with one small window giving natural light to the girl and she can't be seen from the street or by the neighbors. It is near enough to Camp Nou so strangers in the neighborhood don't draw attention."

"Camp Nou?"

"The Barcelona *fútbol* stadium."

"Great, we'll have a bunch of drunks wandering around outside," J Otis said and took a swallow of his vodka.

"You and I will fit right in then."

"Shut up." J Otis didn't want to go down that hole. "Do you know the owner?"

"Yes, he's from Pamplona. His caretaker is letting us in to look around."

"Do you know the caretaker?"

"No, but the owner trusts him."

"Can you trust this caretaker to keep his mouth shut?"

Nuria thought about the question.

"It doesn't matter. He won't be there when we move the girl. He has no reason to be suspicious."

"What about the owner?"

"He's a strong supporter of our cause and he knows everything I do is for the cause."

The limousine driver slammed on the brakes nearly hitting a small boy who ran into the street chasing a soccer ball.

Half the vodka in J Otis' glass splashed onto the floorboard.

"Damn it, that was expensive vodka."

"The house is just up ahead," Nuria said to get J Otis' mind back on what was important.

"I don't like the fact there are kids in the neighborhood. Kids are noisy and nosy. Plus, you can't trust the little vermin."

"Shut up, J Otis." Nuria barked.

There were no available parking spaces in sight so the chauffeur pulled the car up on the sidewalk and shifted into park.

J Otis let Nuria step out first and close her door. He checked the back window then stepped from the car.

"Don't go anywhere," he barked to the chauffeur.

Standing next to the front door smoking a cigarette was a stubby man in his mid-fifties with a noticeable paunch and patches of silver dollar sized bald spots dotting his head.

"Welcome," he said and flicked his cigarette into the street. "I am Oswaldo." He squinted and studied Nuria's face.

Nuria looked away as she shook his hand. "I am Mariu and this is my American friend, Oscar. Thank you for showing us the house."

Oswaldo unlocked the door and walked inside with Nuria on his heels. J Otis stayed outside looking up at the façade.

"Let's go, Oscar," Nuria yelled. "Oswaldo has only a short time to show us around."

J Otis strolled in, ignoring Nuria and Oswaldo as he walked past. He moved through the first floor at a quick pace. When he returned, he said, "Let's go upstairs."

On the second floor, Oswaldo gave a description of the three bedrooms and the large bathroom. He pointed up and said, "On the top level is just one room with a small window. It is a perfect size for a young child's playroom. Do you want to see it."

Nuria shook her head. "We've seen all we need. We'll

take it on a one-week trial. Did you bring the papers?"

Oswaldo patted his sport coat pocket. "We can sign the papers downstairs."

Back down in the living area, Oswaldo placed the papers on a table as he studied Nuria. "You look very familiar. Are you from Bilbao? My wife is from there. Perhaps that is where I've seen you."

Nuria kept her cool. She was a master at hiding her surprise. "I have never been to Bilbao. Perhaps you saw someone who looks like me?"

"Maybe. I am normally very good with faces and I could swear I know you."

"I have a very common face," Nuria replied then coughed. "Could you get me a glass of water? I seem to have something stuck in my throat."

Oswaldo turned and walked to the kitchen.

When she heard the water running in the sink, Nuria slid a serrated knife from her purse and moved silently to the kitchen entrance.

As the caretaker came through the doorway with a glass of water in his hand, Nuria jammed the knife into Oswaldo's stomach and twisted. He dropped the glass. It shattered on the tile floor, water splashing in all directions.

Nuria spun Oswaldo around, grabbed him by his forehead, jerked his head back and slit his throat, all in one motion.

Oswaldo tried to yell for help but only gurgled as blood drooled from his mouth, oozing over his bottom lip.

Nuria released her grip and let Oswaldo drop to the

floor. His legs twitched for a good twenty seconds before going limp as life left his body.

J Otis walked into the doorway. "What the fuck...

"I couldn't take the risk," Nuria said coldly as she searched Oswaldo's pockets for the house keys.

"Shit, now we have to find another place," J Otis said.

"We can still use this place."

She stood and dangled the keys in front of J Otis. "No one will even know we are here."

"What are you going to do with the body?"

"I have someone who will clean it up. When we come back, you won't even know there was a dead body or any blood in here." Nuria walked out. "Let's go get the girl."

The ride back to *El Raval* was funeral parlor quiet. J Otis refreshed his drink and turned away from Nuria. The silence in the limo was broken by Nuria's coughing fit. It lasted a good five minutes. J Otis cracked a window thinking it might help - help him not her.

When they reached the *El Raval* apartment, J Otis gave the chauffeur instructions to return in precisely one hour.

He followed Nuria up the stairs and bumped into her when she suddenly stopped. The high-pitched voice of a man yelling at the top of his lungs echoed down the staircase.

Nuria ran up the stairs. J Otis followed but at a cautious pace. At the top of the stairs Nuria bent over and coughed violently, spitting blood into her hand.

When she finished, she wiped the blood on her pant leg.

She threw open the door to see Nacho standing next to the bed and Jordi standing up on the bed, hovering over Nacho. Jordi's arm was extended, his hand squeezing Nacho's throat.

Layla sat on the far corner of the bed leaning against the wall and hugging her knees to cover herself. She glared at Nuria with defiance in her eyes.

Jordi shot his gaze over to his mother, his eyes widened and his legs began to shake.

"What the hell is going on here?" Nuria screamed.

Jordi released his grip on Nacho's neck and jumped down from the bed. "When I came to relieve Nacho, he was talking sweet things to her." He pointed at Layla. "I could tell they just had sex."

"Go downstairs, Jordi and wait for me. I'll be down in a second."

Jordi leered at Layla and licked his lips.

"NOW, Jordi... go downstairs."

Jordi pointed at Nacho and said, "You can't trust him. He's probably still a cop." When his mother didn't react, Jordi stomped out of the room hyperventilating.

Nuria waited for Jordi to disappear down the stairs before she turned to Nacho.

"Is that true?"

Nacho shook his head vehemently. "You know it's not. Jordi came to relieve me so I could take a short break and use the bathroom. I came back earlier than he expected and found him on top of Layla wrestling with her while he struggled to unzip his pants. He kept saying, 'I just want to play. I just want to play' as he tried to wedge himself between her legs. The little whore fought back hard."

Nuria turned to see Layla nodding her head and staring directly into Nuria’s eyes with chilling contempt.

A shiver ran up Nuria's spine. The look on Layla's face was that of a dangerous, cornered animal.

Nacho stepped in front of Nuria. "That boy of yours is deranged," he said. "He wants to fuck the little whore so bad he can't think straight. Not that he ever could."

Nuria smacked Nacho hard across the cheek. "Don't you ever say that about Jordi. He's not responsible for what he does. You know that. That murderer Kessler is responsible."

J Otis leaned in and waved his hand between Nuria and Nacho. He didn't dare step in between them. "I'm taking the girl with me. It's for the best. She can't be anywhere near your kid."

Nuria pulled the serrated blade from her purse. "It's only the best for you." She said as she stuck the tip of the knife up under J Otis' chin.

J Otis raised his chin as Nuria pushed up on the blade.

She said, "The only way she leaves with you is if you're carrying her dead body over your shoulder or vice versa."

~

CHAPTER 13

Garcia peered around the restaurant averting her eyes from Mack. It was obvious she was deciding how much to tell him about her visit with the *Guàrdia Urbana* cop who was asking around to see whether Mack and Kessler were in Barcelona.

This time Puyol brought just his fingers above the table ledge and wiggled them, signaling for Mack to wait.

"The cop was living in a penthouse apartment no cop can afford. When he saw me, he was overtly nervous and began sweating. I made my visit look routine until I caught him lying to me. When I asked about his background, he said he was from Santander, my hometown. I asked a few questions he couldn't answer then I called him on it. He changed his story and said he was from Pamplona. That was when he pulled a knife. When he raised the knife, I shot him in the forearm, knocking the knife from his hand and him from his chair. I went over to handcuff him so I could begin my interrogation. Before I reached him, he sprung to his feet, ran across the room and then the idiot jumped through the plate glass window. By the time I reached the window, he was lying spread-eagle on the street, seven stories below. A pool of blood was spreading around his head."

Mack studied Garcia's placid expression then pushed his coffee cup away and visualized looking down seven stories at a dead body splayed out on the sidewalk, lying in a pool of blood. He shuddered when he imagined the body hitting the pavement.

It took him a second to realize the look on Garcia's face was one of indifference.

"Why would anyone jump out a window rather than answer some simple questions?" Mack asked.

"Apparently he was dead-set against answering any questions," Puyol replied. "No pun intended."

Mack shook his head in bewilderment.

Garcia said, "The pictures on his walls told me came from a family of cops so any disgrace, misdeed or even suspicion of wrong-doing could drive him to do something extreme, which I think is the case here."

"If that's true, then he had a nefarious reason for inquiring about Kessler and me. That tells me he knew about Layla and her abductors."

"Let's not jump to conclusions just yet. I searched his apartment and found nothing useful. His phone was on him when he jumped so I couldn't get my hands on it." Garcia frowned as if she failed.

She recovered her composure and said, "I called Caroline on my way over and asked her to look into the dead cop. She will send information to Trinity, whoever she is."

"She's a laptop."

Confusion on the two faces sitting across the table from Mack prompted him to explain Trinity and her artificial intelligence.

"A computer that thinks for itself?" Puyol asked. "Where is this world headed?"

"Thinks for *herself*," Mack said. "And let's not go down that road. Let's see what Caroline comes up with on the cop."

Garcia added, "I made another discreet inquiry within the *Guàrdia Urbana*." She saw the concern on Mack's face. "Don't worry about another leak, my contact owes me his life and would never compromise me... never."

The way Garcia said never convinced Mack to never cross her. He'd seen Garcia in action in Rome and was firmly convinced her contact would never dare cross her.

Garcia added, "If he has something, he'll contact me."

The waitress came over with her eyes locked on Puyol. She bent over and seductively winked at him then placed Mack's check on the table. Another button on her shirt was undone.

"I'm off work now so if you could take care of the bill, that would be nice," she said, winked again at Puyol and stood back up.

Mack handed her five Euros. "That's good," he said.

"Thank you," she replied, her eyes never leaving Puyol. She exhaled a despondent sigh and walked away.

Garcia saw the look on Mack's face, admiration for Puyol. She said, "Carles is the most famous footballer to ever come from *Cataluña*. Nothing you can do about that. You both made your living between the white lines. So you, Billy, must remember getting those looks from your days in baseball."

Mack blushed as he said, "I think if we ordered a couple more coffees, she'd be naked. If soccer players have that power, I'm starting to think I should have played soccer instead of baseball."

Garcia shook her head in mock disgust then said, "Let's get back to business. Kessler will land shortly. When he gets here, we analyze all our options. We need to find Layla within the next twenty-four hours. Time is crucial."

Garcia saw the affect her words had on Mack.

"Sorry Billy, we cannot afford to ignore the elephant in the room. Twenty-four hours after getting the ransom call are critical, the possibility of the worst-case scenario playing out grows exponentially."

"I know," Mack replied. He cast his eyes down, staring resolutely at his coffee. "We do what we gotta do."

"Let's go over what we know," Puyol said. "No detail is too small. Then you, Billy, give us your thoughts on why this is happening."

"We've already done that," Mack said.

"And we'll do it as many times as necessary," Garcia

said. She had taken charge.

Mack recounted the kidnapping. He gave a detailed account of the two attempts on him in Switzerland. He generalized about his bad blood with J Otis Weil and ended with the ransom call to his sister.

When he finished, he exhaled and said, "I first thought Layla was kidnapped to get to me. But something is eating at me. What I can't figure out is why the kidnappers are demanding Kessler accompany me at the ransom drop. That doesn't make any sense. He has no connection to Layla or me."

"Ray Gunn would say we have to think outside the box," Puyol said then turned to Garcia. "You know Kessler. Why do you think he's involved?"

"Wait, wait, wait," Mack said, waving his hand in front of his face. He turned to face Garcia directly. "You know Kessler?"

Garcia glared at Puyol then turned her gaze back to Mack. "We worked together for a period of time. We-"

Puyol cut her off, "Maite, you and Kessler more than worked together. You need to put all your cards on the table. Your history, good and bad, with Kessler doesn't matter. Getting Mack's niece back is what matters."

Garcia cleared her throat. "Kessler and I were more than just partners. We were *involved* which was against the rules." She grinned at Mack. "You don't need to know whose rules."

"Is it the same rules Ray Gunn played with?"

"You figure it out."

"Just tell him about you and Kessler," Puyol said.

Mack folded his hands across his chest and sat back.

"I worked with Kessler when he was stationed in Barcelona. Our operation was tasked with rooting out and killing terrorists in Spain, specifically the northern half of Spain. We concentrated on al-Qaeda and ETA, the Basque separatists."

Garcia took another sip of Puyol's espresso.

"We had a mole inside ETA. He gave us intelligence providing a link between al-Qaeda and ETA. The mole had uncovered a plan by ETA to assassinate the top ranking Spanish Admiral, Carlos Gonzalez-Aller Suevos and the American President's top military advisor, General Robert Vorisek at a two-day conference scheduled at the *Palacio Real de Madrid*, the Royal Palace. To divert attention, Al-Qaeda planned to use suicide bombers outside the Palace and at nearby tourist sites. Following the al-Qaeda playbook, the bombs would go off simultaneously. The plan was to wait for the security forces to leave their posts to help with the bombing victims. ETA would then simply walk in and kill both targets. The simplicity was brilliant and probably would have worked had Kessler and I not intervened."

"Intervened?" Mack asked.

Garcia nibbled on the fingernail of her thumb.

She was deciding what she could and couldn't say to him, or to anyone without the proper security clearance. Mack sat back and waited.

"Kessler and I were tasked with apprehending four ETA terrorists before they made it to the Palace. We had eyes on them but were not allowed to move on the targets until the Madrid team assigned to al-Qaeda was operational. One sniff of trouble and al-Qaeda runs away screaming like frightened children. We were ordered to wait until the ETA team was already in Madrid, something Kessler and I were dead set against because it increased the likelihood of innocent bystanders being killed. For ETA, anyone from Madrid was the enemy and if cornered, ETA would start shooting indiscriminately. They welcomed collateral damage."

Garcia paused, reached over and finished Puyol's espresso. She wiped her mouth with a napkin and continued, "Well, the window of opportunity to stop the assassinations was quickly closing so I made an executive decision that if the situation presented itself to take ETA out, dead or alive, regardless whether al Qaeda was on the move or not, we would. Kessler agreed. On the northern outskirts of Madrid, in a suburb called *San Sebastián de los Reyes*, the terrorists made our tail and left the freeway, heading toward a popular shopping center." Garcia grinned. "We let them make us. Long story short, Kessler shot out the back tires and the car crashed into a parked car. Three of the terrorists came out shooting and a one did a rabbit, running into the shopping center. All were dressed in stolen police uniforms. I took out two targets in a shoot-out while Kessler chased after the rabbit. After a game of cat and mouse, the third target, a teenage girl had me in her crosshairs when Kessler returned. He shot her in the back of her leg. She didn't flinch. She spun around and took aim at Kessler. That's when I fired and hit her in the back of her head. She collapsed to the ground but was alive. She bled out and died ten minutes later. The shot to the back of the head made it look like an execution."

"You had Kessler as a witness."

"Kessler didn't officially exist, at least not in Spain. But even if he did, it wouldn't have mattered. It turned out the young girl was the paramour of the Prime Minister. If that became public, he was done. The Prime Minister screwing a sixteen year-old girl was bad enough but she was also an ETA terrorist. I would have been the sacrificial lamb and spent the rest of my days either behind bars or on the run. That's only if someone didn't walk up and put two in the back of my head. It turned out Kessler wasn't going to let that happen."

"But these were terrorists."

"The word 'execution and paramour' are the operative terms here. We had no witnesses to corroborate the truth."

"Did you find out who the rabbit was?"

Garcia shook her head. "I caught of glimpse of him from the side. He or she was a little person who could run. Adding insult to injury, the security cameras at the shopping center were not functioning at the time. A day later, the rabbit was able to anonymously get his or her version of an execution to the authorities and blackmail the Prime Minister, need I say more?"

Puyol cleared his throat then said, "At this point, I think it's important for Billy to know that you and Kessler were under an internal review for your *relationship*. Agents are not permitted to have a *personal relationship* with other agents." Puyol raised his eyebrows as he pronounced *personal relationship*. "It happens all the time but an agent Maite works with had it in for her and was bent on ruining her career."

Garcia interjected, "Our relationship is not the reason I moved to Rome and became and independent contractor, a freelancer. I was burned. It was self-preservation."

Puyol continued, "Kessler knew she would be crucified for disobeying orders and for engaging in a shootout on a public street so the official report had Kessler as the shooter."

Garcia cut in, "I argued with John not to take the fall but he went ahead without telling me. He was secretly expelled from Spain and that ended our relationship. I found out later, the *official* report identified the three dead as bank robbers wanted for a series of hold-ups. The cover-up was already in place and any witnesses would inexplicably disappear. Gunn protected Kessler but didn't have the reach to protect me. I had to disappear myself."

"The powers that be didn't want the public to know there was another terrorist plot, even if it was foiled," Puyol added. "The Prime Minister was especially interested in covering up the facts."

"The report didn't mention that the dead *bank robbers* were from the same family, the infamous Otxoa (pronounced *Oat-cho-A*) family," Garcia said. "I wonder why?"

"What about the rabbit?" Mack asked.

Garcia and Puyol both shrugged their shoulders.

Garcia added, "Kessler and I canvassed the center but came up empty. We couldn't identify ourselves so we said we were looking for mentally disturbed relative of mine who thinks he's a cop."

"Why couldn't you identify yourselves?" Mack asked.

It took Mack a second to grasp that he'd asked Garcia a question she wasn't about to answer.

"When is Kessler arriving?" Garcia asked, changing the subject.

Mack glanced at his watch. "In about an hour."

"Is he staying at the safe house?"

"Yes he is, why?"

"Just curious." Garcia stood from the table and pushed in her chair.

~

CHAPTER 14

Mack's expression told Garcia he expected more of an answer than *'just curious.'*

"I have an errand to run followed by an appointment. See you at the safe house later tonight." Garcia said. She pivoted on her heel and walked away.

As Garcia walked out the restaurant door, Mack recalled the two Iranian agents she'd killed in Rome. Two shots with a silencer and two men dead, both with a perfect kill shot through the head... in the dark of night.

When Garcia turned down the street, Puyol said, "She's going to get her guns and head to the shooting range. She's strange that way. I call her a 'feel' shooter. She will fire each of her weapons and go with the one she was most accurate with today. She changes her weapon of choice as often as she changes her clothes."

"Is there a good reason for her going to the shooting range?"

"It tells me she's expecting trouble within the next twenty-four hours, even if she has to start it."

Puyol led Mack out on the street and did a slow walk back to the safe house. At the front door, he made sure the street was clear then tapped the security code into his phone. The heavy steel door creaked open and the lights inside the house slowly brightened.

Mack stretched out across the sofa and took a nap. When he woke, he retrieved Trinity from atop his overnight bag and opened her up. The screen flickered before growing completely white. A few seconds later, a dark circle appeared in the center and slowly expanded. As it filled the screen, a fuzzy picture materialized and gradually came into focus. A beautiful woman with short, disheveled black hair sat up from a bed. She wore a pair of checkered blue men's pajamas. She stretched her arms over her head and looked directly at Mack. He did a double take. She looked exactly like Caroline but with black hair.

"Sorry Billy, I was napping. Give me a second to get myself together." She snapped her fingers and her pajamas were transformed to a white t-shirt and black yoga pants. She ran her hand through her hair, rearranging the dishevelment. "I'm ready, what are we doing?"

"Do I have any messages from Caroline?"

On the screen, Trinity walked across the floor

rubbing her back as the camera followed her. She sat at her desk.

A strange feeling came over Mack. He felt like a voyeur, a peeping Tom sneaking a peek through the window.

"Before I answer, I have to ask you a favor, Billy."

"Shoot."

"Funny you should use that term. It has to do with being shot. Please, Billy, not to use me as a shield again. When that bullet hit me, it hurt."

"I won't and thank you for taking a bullet for me."

"You're welcome. You have no messages from Caroline."

"That's strange, I expected her to have more info on who made the ransom call."

"She has her people working relentlessly on that. In the meantime, she asked me to dig up some background on that policeman, the one who died from a fall out his seven-story window. His name is Xavier Ybarra *(pronounced E-Barra)*. He was born and raised in Pamplona and moved to Barcelona to join the *Guàrdia Urbana*, the municipal police force. He was a highly decorated officer, has never been married and built a successful on-line side business providing vacation and short-term rental apartments in and around Barcelona. He has over a hundred thousand Euros in his bank accounts and four point two million Euros in investments."

"Does he have any family?"

"Xavier's mother is deceased and buried west of Pamplona in the small village of Iza, her birthplace. She died of a gunshot wound to the head. It was ruled a suicide. His father is alive and lives in Pamplona. He's a former policeman turned politician. He's a member of the municipal council. Rumors abound of an affiliation with the military wing of *Euskadi Ta Askatasuna*, or ETA. Those rumors have never been verified and the man has a stellar reputation in Pamplona and the Basque Country. Xavier had a brother, Ignacio, who is listed as deceased. He was a Pamplona detective who disappeared while investigating a local ETA terrorist ring. His body was never found and there is no death certificate. The police had a missing persons file on him until his father petitioned to have him declared dead. Soon after, the father received a large settlement from the city of Pamplona."

"Is there anything else I should know?"

Trinity smiled at the camera. "I'm glad you asked. The police report has tentatively listed Xavier Ybarra's death, his fall through a seventh story window as murder. Witnesses report an unidentified woman entering the building prior to his death but no one reported seeing her leave. As we speak, they have a team reviewing street cameras for four square miles around Ybarra's apartment. So far, they have nothing. I can promise you they will find nothing." Trinity had a devious look in her eye.

"Thank you and one last question. Do you have a current location for John Kessler and when he's expected at the safe house?"

"John Kessler's plane landed at El Prat Airport fifteen minutes ago. He and Rikki Ryman, the pilot, are entering the Barcelona city limits on the B-20. Their estimated time of arrival is seventeen minutes and twenty-one seconds, given current road conditions."

"Trinity, is there a way for you to alert me when you have anything new to report?"

"Of course. I will send you a text when I have something for you to see. If have information that is vital, I will call you."

"Thank you." Mack rose and walked over to his overnight bag.

"Before you leave, Billy, can you do me a favor and close the screen? I don't like being watched while I work. It creeps me out."

Billy walked back and closed the monitor.

Seventeen minutes and twenty-one seconds later, Mack was in his room when his phone chimed, alerting him he had a text message from Trinity.

John Kessler and Rikki Ryman are outside

"Carles, our guests have arrived," Mack shouted as he entered the foyer.

The front door creaked open. John Kessler filled the doorway. In his right hand was a heavy duffel bag and in his left hand was a small suitcase. He stepped inside, dropped the suitcase and carefully laid the duffel bag down. He turned around and walked back outside.

Kessler returned carrying two heavy Adidas bags, the straps straining under the weight. He dropped the bags in the middle of the foyer.

Rikki Ryman strolled in behind Kessler and nodded to Mack. "Mr. McMillan, nice to see you again."

Before Mack could answer, Rikki turned and hugged Kessler. She kissed him on each cheek then whispered, "It was so great to see you again, John."

She marched out without looking back. The steel door creaked shut behind her.

"Billy Mack," Kessler said, extending his hand. "I read your dossier on the flight over. I feel like I already know you."

Mack stepped back. "There's a file on me?"

Kessler rubbed his baldhead and said. "There's a dossier on everybody who has ever come in contact with Ray Gunn. It's standard operating procedure. We can waste time talking about why there is a dossier on you or we can get down to the business of finding Layla."

Mack knew he was right but couldn't shake the nagging feeling of being violated.

"You're right, the priority is Layla."

"Before we start, where do you want to store the money?" Kessler asked.

The front door creaked as it opened. Maite Garcia stood in the doorway with her arms folded across her chest and a combative expression on her face.

"I never thought I'd live to see this day, John," she said. “Let me restate that. I never thought *you'd* live to see this day.”

She dropped her arms and clenched her fists. "You bastard."

~

CHAPTER 15

J Otis crept up the stairs, stood in the doorway and stared at Layla as she lay on the bed, asleep in the fetal position. Her scent permeated the room: fresh, fragrant and feisty. Just the way J Otis liked.

He'd agreed to watch her while Nacho took a break. He was there to keep Jordi away from her. There was no way he was about to let that scrawny little pervert Jordi near his beautiful young prize.

As he leered at Layla asleep in her bra and panties, he thought of the three million *and one* reasons he wanted her. He was financing her abduction to get back the three million dollars he had *invested* in the Eulalia Society for Girls, money he was convinced Mack had stolen. But it was only partially about the money. He had a more important reason, the *and-one* reason. He wanted Layla for his own. If push came to shove, she was worth three million. He could get three million dollars any time he wanted. It was merely an added bonus to get rid of Billy Mack. That prick had the audacity to steal from him.

Plus when this was over, whether or not he had his money back, he'd take Layla with him to Moscow as his courtesan, his hot, young concubine.

He thought of the added bonus. He smiled as he thought about the pain and agony Billy Mack was going through. "Fuck him," he said under his breath.

Layla opened her eyes and glared at him. She reached down and pulled up on the shackle around her left ankle. She rubbed her swollen left foot then threw the chain away from her leg.

She returned her death stare to J Otis and said, "When Billy comes and rescues me, he's going to kill you. If he doesn't, I will."

Her cold, emotionless tone sent a chill through J Otis. It took him a second to regain his composure.

He inhaled deeply, taking in Layla's scent, then calmly and viciously said, "Billy Mack will be dead as soon as he delivers the ransom. Then you and I will begin our life together... at least until I tire of you or you get too old."

Layla rolled over and turned away from J Otis. She knew from experience in dealing with men like him there was a time to attack and a time to retreat. Lying on a bed, half naked and shackled to the bedpost was a time to retreat... and wait.

"What are you doing here?"

The harsh voice startled J Otis. He slowly turned to see Nuria and Jordi standing two feet behind him.

"I'm keeping an eye on her while Nacho takes a break."

Nuria stepped close to J Otis, an unlit cigarette dangling from her lips. "Time to move to the new place. Jordi will get her ready."

J Otis crinkled his nose as his eyes began to water. He took a small step back to get away from the stench of body odor and cigarettes emanating from Nuria. He said, "Nacho will get her ready and only Nacho." J Otis deliberately avoided looking at Jordi. "Before we move her, you and I are going back to the new place and check it out to assure there is no trace of the body or the blood and no cops around. I want to see with my own eyes."

Nuria lit the cigarette then said, "I was assured the place is clean. We go now... with the girl."

J Otis decided to persuade her with logic. "It will only take an hour for us to check it out. Remember who we're dealing with. Making certain the coast is clear of cops makes sense."

Nuria shook her head side to side as she sucked on the cigarette finishing it in one drag.

J Otis added, "I have someone meeting us there who we can use as a back-up. You'll be glad he's here."

Nuria didn't expect J Otis to bring someone else in. She had to play this out. She blew thick smoke in J Otis's face then said, "Fine, one hour, no more."

"As soon as Nacho returns, we leave."

J Otis pulled Nacho aside and threatened to have his

Russian *fixer* pay Nacho and his family a visit if Jordi gets anywhere near Layla.

"*Entiendo*," Nacho said meekly.

Satisfied Nacho understood, J Otis bounded down the steps saying, "Let's go, my car is waiting outside."

The limo followed the same route back to the apartment near Camp Nou. J Otis replied to text messages as the drove. Nuria fought off a coughing fit then cracked the window and lit a cigarette.

Before they stepped out of the limo, J Otis said, "When my guy shows up, I don't want a repeat of the caretaker, Oswaldo. Do you understand?"

"If it doesn't need to be done, it won't be done."

"You better think twice, he's a *Vor*, a made man in Russia. His family's favorite sport is revenge... slow, relentless revenge." J Otis figured that would make Nuria think twice before she did anything stupid.

Standing near the new hideout's front door was an athletic man in his twenties in a trim black suit, black shirt and black tie. His black hair tied back into a ponytail. His left hand held a bulky black briefcase.

He removed his thick black-framed glasses as J Otis and Nuria approached. "Mr. Weil, Mrs. Oriol, I am Vlad. Like Vlad the Impaler." He laughed as if it was the funniest thing he'd ever heard.

"Thank you for coming, Vlad. We don't have much time so let's get started," J Otis said.

"Get started doing what?" Nuria asked.

"I-" Vlad started to answer then looked at J Otis.

J Otis nodded for him to continue.

"I am to sweep place for bugs and remote cameras. I already make a sweep of surroundings. Is clean."

"Fine," Nuria said and waved him away.

"I start on top floor and work way down. Once I sweep apartment, I re-look street again for anything suspicious. In case you followed."

Vlad climbed the steps two at a time.

"Aren't you happy I called Vlad?"

"Why would I be happy?"

"You can rest assure the place is clean and we won't have to move Layla again."

Nuria fought off a coughing fit and lit another cigarette.

"Do you have your team ready for the ransom drop?" J Otis asked.

"Everything is set. The only thing left is to make the call."

"Walk me through it."

"Why? So another Vlad can appear and take my share?"

"Don't be paranoid. The key to success is preparation."

"Fine. We call Billy Mack from my untraceable satellite phone. We instruct him and Kessler to bring the duffel bags of money to the *Camp Municipal de Beisbal Carlos Pérez de Rozas* where he'll receive a call with further instructions."

"Just tell him the baseball stadium on Montjuic," J Otis said and laughed. "I love the irony of Billy Mack delivering ransom to a baseball stadium then dying there."

"Why is that so funny?"

J Otis was about to explain, stopped and said, "Inside joke, you wouldn't understand. Continue."

"When they are at the stadium, I call with instructions to leave one of the bags of money on the field then they deliver the other bag to the underground parking garage at Sants, the main train station. On the lowest level, there will be a yellow Mini Cooper with a Judas Priest bumper sticker on the back window. Place the bag in the back of the car and wait for the call to tell him where he can find Layla."

"And where is that?" J Otis asked to make sure she had the right location.

"Back at the baseball stadium on Montjuic."

"That is where we kill Billy Mack and take Kessler." J Otis put his arms out wide. "I'm a visionary genius. Who else would kill Billy Mack in a baseball stadium? No one but me. It's the sweetest payback anyone could imagine."

J Otis sensed Nuria was confused. "You have to know Billy Mack to understand."

"Are you done?"

"Remember to tell Mack that we have eyes on him and Kessler the entire time."

"I know what I'm doing, J Otis. This is not my first kidnapping."

Vlad came down the stairs, ignoring J Otis and Nuria as he swept the entire first floor.

Fifteen minutes later, he reappeared, coming out of the kitchen. "Is clean."

Vlad shook J Otis' hand, nodded to Nuria and strolled out the door.

"I told you this place was clean," Nuria said, not hiding her frustration.

"Let's go get Layla," J Otis replied. "Lock the door behind you."

On the drive back to retrieve Layla, J Otis stared out the window as he daydreamed about having Layla with him in Moscow. He imagined her in his bed every night, satisfying his every desire. He would parade her around at his parties and if important guests, such as the Russian President or Prime Minister, were over for dinner, he would share his little prize with them. She will be a huge asset with the rich and powerful in Moscow.

Pulling up to the *El Raval* apartment, the front door to the building was ajar.

J Otis had a bad feeling. He jumped out and sprinted to the door. Nuria passed him as they neared the building. The inside door to the apartment was wide open. Nuria ran in and sprinted up the stairs. J Otis stopped in the living area and surveyed the room. Everything seemed to be in order.

"No, no, no," Nuria screamed from upstairs.

J Otis ran up the stairs to find Nuria standing in the doorway to Layla's room. She was bent over in a coughing fit, her hand over her mouth catching spurts of blood.

Nacho lay on the floor next to the bed, two large cuts across his stomach, his throat slit from end to end and chunk of hair missing as if someone tried to scalp him, the carpet beneath him was soaked in blood.

Layla and her clothes were gone.

~

CHAPTER 16

J Otis raced down the stairs. On the bottom step, he stumbled and fell to his knees. He popped up and looked around. There was no sign of Layla or Jordi anywhere.

Nuria came down the steps grabbing the handrail tightly on each step. Wet blood covered the front of her pants, both legs.

"That little bitch seduced my boy," she screamed, her voice raspy. "That is the only possible explanation."

"Get a grip. That sick little shit took her. We need to find out where."

Nuria tensed at J Otis calling her son a *sick little shit.* She spun on her heels and marched into the kitchen. She yanked the bottle of *DYC Whisky* from the cupboard, unscrewed the cap and chugged from the bottle. The burn in her throat made her forget what J Otis called Jordi. She walked back in the living area holding the bottle by its neck.

J Otis said, "This is a complete cluster fuck. We make the ransom call as if we still have Layla. We arrange for the drop as planned. Once we have the money, we find Jordi and the girl."

"With Nacho dead, we're down one man. How do I get Kessler?"

"I'll talk with Vlad. If he agrees, you'll pay him what he asks."

"We split Vlad's payment, fifty-fifty."

J Otis knew it would look suspicious if he agreed right away. He had to strenuously object then come up with a solution.

"You want Kessler, you pay Vlad what he demands."

Nuria smirked. She had J Otis. "Who's going to kill Billy Mack? Nacho can't anymore. I'm certainly not going to and I know you don't have the *cojones* to do it. That leaves Vlad... Fifty-fifty."

J Otis kept a straight face even though he knew she was right. It took every ounce of willpower he could muster to hold his gaze. Layla was worth it but he couldn't agree just yet. Nuria was overly suspicious by nature. She couldn’t suspect Vlad was there for any other reason than to kill Mack and take Kessler. He shook his head like he was disgusted with himself for capitulating.

"On one condition. If I don't get Layla back, you pay Vlad's entire fee. Your kid killed Nacho and took my girl, that's on you."

Nuria set the bottle on a small table next to the wall.

"Fine," she said, staring at J Otis while imagining him lying in a pool of his own blood, vomit and waste when she had him killed. She had one concern: how to handle Vlad. How could she find out if Vlad's family back in Moscow knew she was partnering with J Otis? If anything went sideways, she didn't need the Russian Mafia invading Barcelona.

"I'm glad to see you've come to your senses," J Otis said in a condescending manner.

"Fuck you, J Otis. Call Vlad and arrange for him to get his ass here. I'll make a few calls to see if I can find Jordi and that little bitch."

Nuria took the satellite phone and headed outside, away from J Otis. Out on the street, she faced the open door in case J Otis came down to listen in. She couldn't have him overhearing her conversation.

On the second ring, Nuria's call was answered.

"What's wrong?"

She knew she couldn't sound worried so she kept a self-assured tone in her voice. "We have a small glitch. There is a problem with Nacho, so you will have to step up and kill J Otis once I get Kessler."

"I wasn't hired to kill anyone. I'm only keeping a close eye on J Otis so when the time is right to distract him, Nacho can take him out."

"The deal has changed... obviously. I can order you to do it but I'd rather you volunteer."

The voice on the other end of the line snickered softly, not hard enough to piss off Nuria.

"Volunteer is not the right word. Let's say I step up and kill J Otis. Then you agree to the following terms: My fee increases to two-hundred and fifty thousand and when this is over, I take Kessler. I need to curry favor with our boss. That is, after I eliminate J Otis and take his money."

"As long as I get to kill Kessler. I will text you once the ransom drop is underway."

"One more thing, Neria. Where did your boy take the girl?"

"How... how," Nuria stuttered, "how the hell do you know that? And, it's Nuria."

The voice snickered again. "While you and your partner went to the new hideout, I kept an eye on the apartment. Twenty minutes after you left, your kid came out holding the girl by the arm and a knife pressed against her back. She was barefoot. A few blocks down the street they came to a shoe store, went in for a few minutes and when they came out, the girl was wearing a cheap pair of sandals. Then they took off. The girl was struggling until Jordi whispered in her ear. Her entire body went limp, defeated."

"You followed them? Where are they?" Nuria asked.

"You don't know? He's your son."

"I wouldn't have asked if I knew where they went."

"I lost them outside La Sagrada Familia."

"Where do you think they were headed?"

"Your guess is as good as mine. He's your kid so if anyone thinks like him, it's you, only you."

Nuria ignored his comment. "Wait for my call." She hung up, her eyes still watching the doorway for J Otis. She lit a cigarette, looked up and down the street then marched inside.

Upstairs in the apartment, she faced J Otis. "Is Vlad the Impaler in board?"

J Otis nodded then asked, "What are we doing with Nacho's body?"

"After we leave, my cleaner will fix the place. Once he's done he'll call the police and say he saw a man fitting Kessler's description running out of the building with blood on his hands."

"I like it," J Otis said.

"Of course you do," Nuria said. She wiggled the phone in J Otis' face. "Kessler and Billy Mack are in Barcelona. Time for us to call your friend Billy Mack."

"What if he demands to talk to Layla? What are you going to say?"

"Listen and learn."

~

CHAPTER 17

Maite Garcia stepped into the safe house, her eyes never leaving Kessler. She stood close to him and lifted her head. Kessler was six-foot three with wide shoulders and Garcia was five-foot six and athletically slim.

Mack wasn't sure who would win in an altercation, physical or mental. Garcia's body was tense, like a lioness ready to attack her prey. Kessler widened his stance like a linebacker about to tackle the ball carrier.

"You son-of-a-bitch," Garcia said and slapped him hard across the face, leaving a red mark.

"I wasn't given a choice. I did what I had to do," Kessler replied. "And leave my mother out of this."

"You should have asked me before you did what you did, you bastard."

"If I didn't cop to the shootings and have it reflected in the official report, you would have been public enemy number one with ETA and the spineless politicians in Madrid. I was protected, you weren't."

Garcia chewed on her lip. She didn't expect Kessler's answer. She reached up and swatted him weakly on the cheek. "You should have told me before you left. You owed me that much."

Kessler leaned down and hugged Garcia. He whispered, "They wouldn't let me. I had to leave on the next plane or you were dead. As I boarded the plane, I was ordered never to contact you."

Garcia took a step back. "Who gave you the order?"

"It was relayed to me by my boss."

"Ray Gunn?" She studied Kessler's face.

Kessler kept his gaze directly on Garcia's eyes.

"Did Gunn give you the name?" Garcia asked in a subdued voice.

"He said it came from the highest levels of your governments and left it at that."

A confused look washed over Garcia's face. "Then why are we both here now?"

"Gunn said he wouldn't allow a politician to get in the way of saving a young girl's life. He'll run interference if the wrong people learn we are in Spain." Kessler raised his eyebrows.

Garcia punched Kessler in the stomach, just hard enough for him to react. "I owed you that."

"Fair enough."

Mack cut in, "Save your class reunion for later. We only have a day to find Layla and get her to safety."

"Where's Carles?" Garcia asked.

"I'm right here," Puyol said as he walked into the foyer. "Let's move this into the kitchen. I have *tapas,* or appetizers in English, set out if anyone is hungry."

"What about the money?" Kessler asked, pointing to the two duffel bags.

"The bags are safe where they are," Puyol replied.

The modern kitchen had dark gray granite countertops, light gray cabinets and a large island in the center. A brushed-steel table stood near the wall. The stainless steel appliances were top shelf.

In the kitchen, Mack walked over to the island, loaded a small plate with thinly sliced ham and four cheese *croquetas*. He sat at the table and popped a *croqueta* into his mouth. Garcia and Kessler avoided the food and sat opposite Mack. Puyol grabbed a can of beer from the refrigerator and sat next to Mack.

"I expect to receive the ransom instructions any time now," Mack said. He pointed at Kessler then himself. "My gut tells me Kessler and I are being set up. Once the call comes, we have a very small window to come up with a plan."

"When dealing with kidnappers," Kessler said, "it's essential to speak with the abductee at regular intervals, no matter what ransom or other instructions are given. It reduces the odds of the kidnappers..." He looked uneasily at Mack. "Disposing of any evidence."

"That's easier said than done," Garcia added.

"Under the circumstances, we must assume you two are being watched at all times," Puyol said. "At least from the time the ransom is delivered."

Garcia agreed. She added, "The kidnappers will assume Billy and John have people in Barcelona assisting them. They just don't know who."

"We can't assume they don't know who," Mack said.

"The only people who know Carles and I are involved are you two and Ray Gunn."

Kessler shook his head. "Rikki Ryman and the driver of the Suburban also know."

"Let me correct myself," Garcia said. "The only people who know I'm involved are you three and Ray Gunn."

"I know you prefer to work alone Maite, but don't cut me out of this based on that assumption," Puyol said.

Garcia stood from the table and strolled over to the food set out on the island counter. As she placed a medley of *tapas* on her plate, she said, "I'm not in any way trying to cut you out. Given we have a very short window to get Layla, you and I must work separately. That's all I'm saying."

"That makes sense," Kessler said. "Carles, your face is one of the most famous in Barcelona so you can't be seen anywhere near the ransom drop. You know that."

"I wasn't planning on showing my face."

Mack stood up and walked toward the foyer. He said, "Keep talking, I'll be right back."

Kessler strolled over the refrigerator and grabbed a can of beer. He popped it open as he walked back to the table, took a drink from the can then said, "I forgot how good Spanish beer is."

"Catalan beer." Puyol said and grinned.

"I forgot, *nuestro país*," Kessler replied.

"That's right, *our country*."

"Sorry, I forgot how good *Catalan* beer is."

Mack walked in carrying Trinity in front of him, the screen up at a ninety-degree angle. He gently placed Trinity on the table and turned her so everyone viewed the screen.

"Tell everyone what you told me, Trinity."

"I will dispense with the greetings and get right to what we know." Trinity paused briefly as a black and white headshot filled the screen.

"This is Xavier Ybarra, the policeman who is reported to have been thrown from a seventh story window even though there is no evidence in the police report. He has an interesting background. He was a decorated cop and successful entrepreneur, or so the police believe. I did some forensic accounting and found that the seed money for his start-up business of vacation rentals in and around Barcelona came from questionable sources in Pamplona and Bilbao. I say questionable because the money he received from Pamplona came through his father's bank account. It was only in his father's account for one day. That's what I call a poor attempt at money laundering. The money from Bilbao came from a small company called *Compañía de Jordi*. That company is connected to the notorious Otxoa family. The origin of that money is from a charity. There is strong circumstantial evidence the charity is a money laundering front for ETA and al-Qaeda. I am searching for concrete evidence the father knew this."

Mack rubbed his chin in thought. "Trinity, can you generate a list of all the vacation rentals Ybarra owned in

Barcelona?"

"Of course, anything for you, Billy." The screen flickered and a list of properties replaced the headshot of Ybarra. "Here is the list separated by districts."

"Bring up *El Raval*," Mack said.

A list of ten properties appeared on the screen.

"How many are listed as vacant?"

Five properties appeared on the screen.

"Can you separately check all cameras, traffic or otherwise in the area of each apartment," Kessler asked, "and run facial recognition for Xavier Ybarra, J Otis Weil and anyone associated with them, here and in Europe?"

"Of course, John. But, it will take a little time to run the program."

Mack's phone rang. The caller ID on the screen read 'UNKNOWN.'

"It's the kidnappers."

~

CHAPTER 18

Mack lifted his phone from the table, stared at it then tapped the green button on the screen. He glanced at his watch. It was after midnight. "Why are they calling now?" he mouthed then pointed to Trinity. He held his hand over the phone.

"Have Trinity trace this call," he whispered.

He removed his hand from the phone. "Billy Mack," he said.

"Shut the fuck up and listen." The female voice had a harder edge to it this time. Mack felt hostility and hatred radiating from the phone.

The ransom instructions were terse and concise. He would receive further instructions after the drop was made.

When she finished she said, "I am in charge and you do as I say. You follow, *cabrón*?"

The tone of voice was now brash and buoyant to the extent Mack sensed a hint of glee in her words.

Mack steeled himself and said, "Before I pay any ransom I talk to Layla. Put her on the phone."

"You didn't say pretty please."

Mack bit his lip. He knew he had to play her game. "Pretty please."

"Too late. Maybe next time."

The phone line went dead.

Mack dropped his phone on the table. "Did we get a trace?"

Kessler turned the laptop toward Mack.

Trinity's face appeared on the screen. There was sadness in her eyes. "Sorry, Billy, I couldn't get an exact location. The call came from a satellite phone with its GPS disabled. I was able to use the Doppler shift from the satellite but only have a proximity. The call was made from the *El Raval* neighborhood of Barcelona. Because of the brevity of the call, I can only say the call was made near the Mediterranean Sea, no more than half a kilometer away. If she calls again, I can further hone the location."

"Thank you, Trinity."

"Caroline was more successful. She embedded an eavesdropping program on the satellite phone, a program developed by Nimesh at Mira Labs. It allows me to remotely activate the microphone on the phone, even when the phone isn't being used."

"Can you record the conversations?"

"Yes, I have a digital recorder connected to the program and will send the recordings to your phone after every conversation."

"Can you think of anything else?" Mack asked then realized he just requested a computer to think for itself, or in this case, herself.

"I am checking all the cameras in and around *El Raval* and running my facial recognition program. Narrowing the grid will speed up my search." Trinity rubbed her eyes like she was tired. "Let me get back to work."

Mack slowly closed the computer screen.

Kessler marched over to the refrigerator, grabbed two cans of beer and tossed one to Mack.

Mack's hand shot up, catching the can over his left shoulder. He placed the can on the table in front of him. He said, "It was the same woman who called. Tomorrow we are to deliver both bags of money to the baseball field on Montjuic."

Mack popped open the can, looked at Puyol and asked, "You have a baseball field in Barcelona?"

"It was for the Olympics. Montjuic was the main Olympic site."

"Are you or Maite familiar with it?"

Garcia nodded and said, "The baseball stadium is near the Sant Jordi Arena and the Olympic football, I mean soccer stadium. There is only one road in and out to the drop. The stadium has an exterior fence that's easily breached. Why are you asking?"

"Tomorrow at noon, Kessler and I are to each carry a bag and bring the money to the stadium, place the bags on the pitcher's mound and wait for instructions." Mack said then stood and pushed his chair from the table.

"Hold on," Kessler said and waited for Mack to sit back down. "We need to talk about this. You didn't speak with Layla so we don't know her condition... her situation. If the kidnappers want the money, you make it contingent upon you speaking with Layla."

"How do I do that? I can't call the woman back."

"No, but you can show up without the money. When she calls with further instructions, demand to talk to Layla before you release the money."

"I don't know. That's risky."

"I'll have the money nearby with Carles as my back-up. I can get the bags to you in no time."

"Before we over-think this," Garcia said, "we need to answer a few questions."

"Such as?" Kessler asked.

"Why is the money to be in delivered in two duffel bags? Why are John and Billy each carrying a bag? Why is the location drop in a wide-open public space? *Montjuic* always has a crowd. But..." Garcia raised her finger and shook it at Mack. "The question that really bothers me is this: Why didn't she let you speak with Layla? We must know if she is... We need to know her situation."

Mack didn't like the last question and Garcia's response. He brought the can of beer to his lips and took a drink.

“I'll take one bag of money with me as an enticement.”

Kessler thought about Mack's idea as he popped open his can of beer. “I agree. It'll reduce the pissed-off factor and it gives us a better chance to call an audible."

"Audible? Puyol asked. He took a sip of his beer as waited for someone to explain.

"Basically, a change of plans," Kessler replied.

"You've each had your last can of beer or any alcohol until we get Layla back, understood?" Garcia ordered.

Mack, Kessler and Puyol nodded in unison.

"Good, now here's what I think we should do. Chime in if you disagree with any of it."

Garcia laid out a detailed plan with specific contingencies. When she finished, she said, "Let's sleep on it and reconvene early tomorrow morning."

~

CHAPTER 19

Nuria hung up the satellite phone and burst into a relentless coughing fit. She covered her mouth. Blood and phlegm splattered into the palm of her hand. She wiped her hand on her pant leg and snatched the bottle of whiskey off the small table. She drank slowly from the bottle letting the whiskey burn replace the pain in her lungs.

"Did Vlad agree?" she asked as she lit a cigarette. A trickle of blood and phlegm seeped from the corner of her mouth and ran down her chin.

J Otis turned his head away. He said, "I went through the operation with him and he's up to speed. He'll kill Mack and deliver Kessler to where you want for a hundred grand. It he's forced to kill Kessler, that's another hundred grand."

"Agreed. Does he know our timing?"

"He'll be in place tomorrow morning at ten."

Nuria wiped the blood and phlegm off her chin then sucked her cigarette down to the butt. She exhaled a thick plume of smoke, dropped the butt and ground it into the floor with her toe.

She said, "Did you tell him not to go near the baseball stadium until we know Mack and Kessler are on their way? They may have eyes moving into the area now. I can't have any more glitches from here on out."

"He's a pro, he knows what to do."

"Is that a yes or a no?"

"That's a yes. I went over the plan with him."

Nuria took a swig of whiskey then said, "I'm going up to take a shower."

"About time," J Otis whispered.

"You can see yourself out. Be back here at nine tomorrow."

J Otis strolled out, slamming the door behind him.

Nuria walked over to the window and watched J Otis crawl into his limo and drive away. As the rear lights of the limo faded from view, Nuria took another swig and thought about her contingency plan to protect her from J Otis and Vlad, *just in case*. If Vlad stayed loyal to J Otis, she'd need someone watching her back. If Vlad failed in his duties, she'd need someone to take his place.

One kilometer north of *El Raval* and four blocks west of La Sagrada Familia, Jordi pulled Layla up the dark stairs and into a studio apartment overlooking a quiet street. It was Nacho's apartment and he wouldn't need it anymore.

He flicked on the light. On the left was a small café table and two chairs standing near a kitchenette. Two tattered wing chairs faced the opposite wall. To the right, a double bed was pushed against the sidewall. Faded yellow paint covered the walls. Halfway up the center of the main wall was a large black and white photo of a shirtless man with his jeans half unzipped. He's holding a sledgehammer over his shoulder.

Jordi shoved Layla across the room to the bed. He tied her arms to the bedposts and walked around the room pulling down the shades.

He strutted back to the bed, pulled his shirt over his head and dropped it next to the bed.

"You are so pretty. I see the way you look at me. I know you want to play with me. You and I are going to have fun tonight. With mother not here, we can play all night."

~

CHAPTER 20

Layla pulled her legs up to her chest and turned her entire body away from Jordi. She twisted toward the wall until her arms couldn't take it anymore and concentrated on a grease spot high up on the wall. It looked like an angel with her wings falling off.

She felt his weight on the mattress as he climbed on the bed. Every muscle in her young body stiffened.

"Please don't," she pleaded, "I beg you."

"I know you want to play with me. I see the way you look at me. You can't take your eyes off me."

Layla wanted to scream. Instead, she kept a wary eye on him but didn't dare utter a peep. In her mind, she was screaming, *"Because you are an evil, sick half-wit who doesn't know right from wrong."*

Jordi grabbed her hip and pulled with all his might to twist her onto her back. It took three strong tugs to get Layla onto her back. As soon as he let go, Layla sprung back into her twisted position, facing the wall.

Jordi crawled closer. This time he grabbed the top of her jeans and pulled. When he had Layla on her back, he gripped the front of her jeans, undid the top button and pulled down the zipper. He yanked her jeans down, ripped them off her legs and threw them across the room. Layla immediately contorted her body back into her defensive position.

Jordi stood on the bed, grabbed her legs and twisted. The pain in Layla's legs was excruciating and when she couldn't take the torture any longer, her legs went limp and Jordi flipped her onto her back.

He jerked off her panties then dropped to his knees and pushed her shirt up and over her bra. He ripped off her bra as a demonic smile graced his face. His eyes were no longer looking at her. They were looking through her.

Layla decided to try another tactic.

"Wait, let me get comfortable so we can both enjoy this."

Jordi jumped up on the bed and frantically undid his pants, pulled them down and kicked them off his legs. He sneered down at Layla like a boxer gloating over his downed opponent.

Layla arched her back and with every ounce of strength she could muster, she moaned seductively and tensed her body like a taut spring.

Jordi started to get excited, his lips and chin wet with spittle. A line of drool ran down his chin.

Suddenly, Layla kicked up with all her strength, landing a mighty blow with her right foot directly up into Jordi's testicles.

Jordi's eyes rolled to the back of his head. He teetered left, caught his balance then fell to the right, hitting his head on the bedpost. He bounced off the mattress and landed on the floor with a thud.

Layla tried everything to loosen the ropes tied tightly around her wrists, pulling as hard as she could each time. On her last attempt, she felt her skin tear and blood trickle down her arm. After thirty minutes, she finally gave up.

Exhausted, Layla fought to keep her eyes open while Jordi lay unconscious on the floor. In her mind, she repeated over and over: Stay awake, be ready. Stay awake, be ready.

~

As the early morning sun lit up the cheap yellow shades, Layla awoke feeling a hand on her thigh. She kept her eyes closed and concentrated on the sounds around her. She could hear, feel and smell Jordi close to her. He was breathing rapidly and mumbling to himself in a language Layla didn't understand. It sounded like he was speaking in tongues.

Layla cracked one eye to see Jordi lying right next to her. He was naked. He was inches away, staring into her eyes. His left hand rested on her thigh while his right hand vigorously rubbed his groin area. It was like he was unsure where exactly to rub himself.

Jordi's right hand stopped abruptly when he saw

Layla's eye partially open. A stupid grin surfaced and his cheeks grew crimson.

"Play with me."

Layla eyes moved down to Jordi's groin and thighs. The entire surface was either bright pink or dark red. He'd been rubbing himself for quite some time. She searched her mind for an answer that wouldn't set him off.

"If there is something wrong with you, we should get you to the hospital," she said. Her body was poised to fight back any way possible.

Jordi slapped her hard across the face. "There is nothing wrong with me." He slapped her again, this time harder. "I won't tell mother what you said because she would kill you."

Layla grimaced and tried not to react. She said, "How can I play with you when you can't even play with yourself?"

Jordi jumped off the bed and leaned over until his nose touched Layla's nose. He said, "Mother was right about you. You're a little bitch."

Jordi retrieved his clothes from the floor and hastily dressed. As he walked to the door, he looked over his shoulder and said, "Don't go anywhere." As he grabbed the door handle, he laughed hysterically.

Layla pulled herself up into a seated position and concentrated on the knots Jordi had tied to see how she could loosen them before Jordi returned.

~

In his penthouse suite at the Hotel Arts Barcelona, J

Otis placed his glass of vodka on the table and dug out his encrypted Russian cell phone from his suitcase. He had to make a call to Moscow.

Standing at the window, peering down on early morning lights of Barcelona, he tapped the speed dial number on the screen.

"Hello Arkady, it's your favorite American."

"In your dreams, J Otis. Selma Hayek is my favorite American."

J Otis wasn't sure if Arkady was joking. "Good choice. I was calling to thank you for sending Vlad."

"What do you want, J Otis? You are not calling me to say thank you. You never say thank you unless you want something."

J Otis wanted to correct him but nobody contradicted Arkady - not if they wanted to wake up the next morning.

"Vlad has been invaluable to me and I want to use his services on another project, shall we say."

"You are calling on the encrypted phone Vlad gave you, right?" It wasn't posed as a question.

"Of course. I would never expose myself or you."

"What do you want Vlad to do?"

"I need him to eliminate two problems I have."

"Did you already ask Vlad?"

J Otis realized he was on a slippery slope. In his haste to get Vlad on board, he neglected to consider Arkady.

Another thing you don't do to Arkady is lie to him. "Yes, I asked him only to see if he would be willing to take the job. He told me to talk to you."

"He's a smart boy, much smarter than you J Otis. You should have come to me first."

"That was always my plan. I only asked Vlad because if he said no, I would not have to bother you with my request."

"If you want my people, you come to me first. I decide what my people do or don't do. Vlad does what I tell him. He's a smart boy, that is why he told you to call me."

"It won't happen again."

"If it does, it will be your last time."

J Otis had heard that matter-of-fact tone in Arkady's voice before. The last person he directed it at was never seen from again. "I promise," J Otis said, trying to muster as much confidence as he could.

"I will speak to Vlad then call you back."

"I need to know by-"

The connection went dead.

~

CHAPTER 21

At five a.m., Mack pulled himself out of bed. He'd barely slept, thinking about Layla and the ransom drop, which he was now convinced more than ever was a set-up.

He'd stared up at the ceiling all night with the eerie sense that Layla was suffering beyond imagination. He couldn't erase the terrible thoughts of what could be happening to her. What she was going through no sixteen year-old should. He tossed and turned all night from the recurring nightmare that he'd never see her again.

He pulled on his running shorts and running shirt then tied his running shoes tighter than usual. He strapped the armband holding his phone onto his left bicep and did a cursory stretch before heading to the kitchen for some water. A good run would clear his head.

Walking into the kitchen, he smelled fresh coffee. Puyol sat at the table, a steaming cup of coffee in his hand and the soccer newspaper *SPORT* laid out in front of him. Next to the paper was a small iPod and white wrap-around headphones. He was dressed to work out.

"Do you want a coffee before you go for your run?" Puyol asked.

"I usually wait until after."

Puyol stood from the table. "You know you're going on what you American's call a wild goose chase."

"Better than just sitting and waiting."

Puyol stuck his headphones in his ears. "Mind if I join you on your run? I could use the company."

Mack frowned. "I run alone."

"It wasn't a request. Ray Gunn figured you'd go for a run and I am to accompany you. He said to tell you it isn't negotiable."

Mack rolled his eyes.

Puyol chuckled. "He also said that would be your reaction." He clipped his iPod to his waistband. "I'm not going along as your babysitter. I can lead you to where you want to go much faster."

Mack noticed Puyol's shoes were untied. "Fine, lace 'em up and let's go."

"If you're going to listen to music, keep the volume low enough so we can talk," Puyol said.

Mack nodded as he slipped the ear buds into his ear.

"What do you listen to when you run?" Puyol asked.

"Today it's *Echo and the Bunnymen*. How about you?"

"A mix of *Jarabe de Palo* and *Héroes Del Silencio*."

~

Puyol led the way to *Via Augusta*, a main artery cutting through the city. The street runs from the base of *Tibidabo*, the mountain over-looking the city, down toward the sea and ending at *Avinguda Diagonal*, the wide, tree-lined boulevard bisecting the entire city, east to west.

At five-thirty, the only cars on the road were black and yellow taxis. A full moon hung over the city providing natural light. As a result, the streetlights glowed a lazy yellow.

"*Via Augusta* will take us near *El Raval*, assuming that's where you're headed." Puyol grinned facetiously as he flicked his thumb and pointed down the street.

"Shut up and run," Mack replied as he fought back a smile.

When they came to *Avinguda Diagonal*, they slowed to gage the traffic then crossed the wide road and resumed their normal pace heading to *El Raval*.

"About a half kilometer down from here is the *El Raval* neighborhood," Puyol said. "I will bring us in from the north and make our way down to the sea. That way we can cover the entire neighborhood."

Puyol took off in a sprint, a wide smile growing on his face. Mack was not about to be outdone. He kicked it into high gear, caught Puyol but could not overtake him. Every time he tried, Puyol sped up.

Puyol finally slowed to a walk and held up his hand for Mack to slow. When Mack came up next to him, Puyol held his arms out wide.

"This is *El Raval*. The neighborhood runs from here

down to the Mediterranean."

Mack gazed down at the shabby five-story buildings lining each side of the empty street. Up and down the narrow street, lights began to pop on as workers rose to meet the day.

Puyol led Mack to the end of the street, past a roundabout and down to a large patch of grass with a row of concrete ping-pong tables spaced out across the park.

A police car with its lights flashing zipped past, turned sharply left then sped up as it drove along the park. A block past the park, Mack saw a collection of police cars scattered on the street, lights flashing, blocking traffic.

"What do you think is happening?" Mack asked.

"Stay here, I'll go find out," Puyol answered.

"You think that's wise?"

"How else are we going to find out?" Puyol said as he walked away.

Mack leaned against the wire fence surrounding the park and tried to act casual.

Puyol made the rounds shaking hands with every cop. There was a wide smile on every cop's face. A tall detective in a dark gray suit and brown shoes pushed his way through the crowd of uniformed cops and pulled Puyol aside. The detective spoke non-stop for five minutes during which he handed two sheets of paper to Puyol.

Puyol kept his head down and his eyes on the paper as the detective spoke. When the cop's lips stopped moving, Puyol handed the sheets back to the detective, shook his hand and strolled back to Mack.

Approaching Mack, Puyol avoided eye contact. "Get around the corner and I'll tell you what I learned," he said, worry in his voice.

The expression on Puyol's face twisted a knot in Mack's gut. The image Layla's dead body lying on the ground came into his mind and the knot tightened.

Turning the corner, Puyol looked back at the swarm of police officers as if he didn't want them to see him with Mack.

"They found a dead body in the top floor of that apartment building."

"Male or female?" Mack asked, praying it wasn't Layla.

"Male."

Mack blew a sigh of relief, the knot in his stomach loosened a bit. "Aren't murders rare in Barcelona?"

"Yes, but that's not why there are so many cops here. The dead body they found is a former policeman from Pamplona. His throat was slit from ear to ear. The strange thing is that the records listed him as already deceased. According to the records, he's been dead for a number of years. But that's not the only strange twist. The apartment where they found the body is owned by the dead man's brother, a Barcelona policeman."

Mack opened his mouth to say something.

Puyol held up his hand for Mack to wait. "It gets stranger. The dead man's brother was murdered yesterday, thrown from a seventh story window."

"His brother?" Mack stuck his head around the corner and eyed the cops mulling around at the other end of the block. "Do they have a suspect?" Mack asked, hoping Puyol wouldn't say Garcia.

"Not for the cop thrown from his window."

"How about this murder?"

Puyol flicked his eyebrows up twice. "The cops received an anonymous tip identifying the killers for this murder." Puyol pointed over his shoulder with his thumb, in the direction of the cops down the street. "The primary suspect is a tall foreigner with wide shoulders, who was speaking American English to his accomplice as they ran from the apartment. Both men had blood on their clothes. The detective said they didn't find any blood in the apartment. They figure the killers took the time to clean up. The fact the entire apartment was scrubbed of any evidence by a professional has the entire Barcelona police department on high alert and focusing their efforts on finding or killing the suspects."

"They have eyewitnesses?" Mack asked skeptically.

"The detective wasn't specific. The *Guàrdia Urbana* received an anonymous call. The caller claimed he heard the tall suspect call his accomplice 'Billy Mack.' We better get back, lie low until the ransom drop."

"I'm definitely being set-up," Mack replied.

Puyol replied, "You and Kessler."

Mack wasn't paying attention to Puyol. He eyed the cop cars down the street and said, "Layla was here. I can feel it."

Another cop car with its lights flashing drove past. Puyol stepped in front of Mack to hide him from the white cop car. Mack turned his head away.

The cop car slammed on its brakes.

Puyol shoved Mack behind a dumpster and said,

"Stay along the wall and hurry around the corner. Whatever you do, stay out of sight."

The cop car backed up. Puyol turned around and walked over to the cop car. He placed his hands on the roof of the car to block the driver's sight. He leaned down and waited for the car window to open.

In blue-collar Catalan he said, "Good morning, officers." He turned his head toward the swarm of cop cars down the street. "This is a rare site in Barcelona even for this part of town."

"Carles Puyol, what are you doing down here? This is not the part of Barcelona I would expect to find you."

Puyol smiled comfortably. "I was on my morning run down to the sea when I saw all the commotion over there. I guess I was curious."

"Where did your friend go?"

Puyol gave the cop a confused look like he was trying to figure out what he meant. He mustered an air of surprise. "Oh that guy, he was just some jogger I ran into. He was watching your buddies down the street when I arrived. I barely talked to him."

The cop held up a sheet of paper with Mack's picture next to Kessler's. "That jogger resembled this man." The cop pointed to the headshot of Mack.

Puyol shook his head. "I don't see it."

~

CHAPTER 22

Nuria awoke with a jolt. She thought she'd heard a noise and hurried downstairs hoping to find Jordi and the little bitch. The apartment was empty. She checked the entire floor then marched over to the window and pulled open the curtains. The street was empty and there were only two lights on in the neighboring building. The clock on the wall said six o'clock.

She lit a cigarette and snatched the satellite phone off the table. She had to make this call and nervously punched in the number she knew by heart. Calling Zigor, her boss and the head of ETA's military wing with bad news was like painting a bull's-eye on your forehead. Waking him this early made it even more precarious.

"*Dígame*," came a gruff voice on the other end of the

line.

"Why are you speaking Spanish, *Jefe*? We speak Euskara *(Basque)*, never forget."

"You're being insubordinate again, Neria... Nuria. I don't need a lecture from someone who reports to me."

Nuria calmed her voice. She needed Zigor. "We must refrain from using names. That being said, I have some bad news about your contribution to our cause."

Zigor cut her off, "I received the call from the *Guàrdia Urbana*."

A chilling silence followed and Nuria braced herself for either a fit of rage or tormented grief.

"They will be delivering Xavi's body to a funeral home near here," Zigor said with no emotion.

"What happened to... to X?"

"He was thrown through his apartment window. I'm looking into it."

"I don't believe we're talking about the same person," Nuria said, her voice trembling. "I... I'm talking about your other soldier, the... the one with me," Nuria stuttered. "He was found in the apartment with his throat cut." She paused and waited for Zigor's reaction.

There was another chilling silence on the other end of the line.

Thirty seconds later, Nuria asked, "Are you still there, *Jefe*?"

"Was he alone at the apartment?"

"Yes, we were concerned the apartment was compromised so we secured a new location. Everyone and everything was moved. N stayed behind to clean up, leave no trace. When he was late coming to the new place, I went back and found police cars out front. It is obvious our location was compromised."

"Tell me what you know."

Nuria had to play dumb until she confirmed the cleaner made his call to the police implicating Kessler. But, she had to plant a seed in Zigor's mind implicating Kessler.

"I have people checking into N's murder." Nuria paused for effect then spoke slowly, punching out her words. "I've come into... some interesting intelligence... you need to hear." She paused longer this time, finally releasing a long, exhaustive breath. "The American is back in Barcelona. He and a partner have been in town for a few days. Perhaps they learned of our location and he and his accomplice brutally murdered N while searching for the girl."

Nuria wracked her brain trying to remember what she did and didn't tell Nacho. There was a chance Nacho gave Zigor updates on the kidnapping while she and J Otis were at the new hideout. She had to keep her story vague, have plausible deniability in case Zigor made calls to his contacts in Barcelona and was told something different.

"Either he learned of our location and when he arrived he surprised N or there is some connection to my partner?"

"That doesn't make sense. You told me you covered your tracks."

"Yes *Jefe*, but my partner is a talker. Maybe-"

Zigor cut in, "Talk to your partner, find out what he knows and who he talked to. I want to be kept in the loop at every turn, you understand?"

"I'm waiting to hear from a contact in the *Guàrdia Urbana.* As soon as I know something, you'll know it."

"I will make the necessary calls."

Nuria didn't expect Zigor's reply and scrambled. "Don't make any calls until you hear from me. It may jeopardize my contact's position inside the force. Besides, I need a favor from you."

"It better be critical. I have a body is being delivered tomorrow morning and now I have to make arrangements for another."

"It is critical. N was an important part of the team and I... we need to replace him?"

"You already have my best *trigger man* watching your back."

It was as if a ton of bricks just fell on Nuria. When she'd spoken with Kelmen earlier, she forgot to ask him about Nacho. She had to play this out carefully.

"And he is doing his usual exceptional job. But I am now short-handed. I could really use another body to help."

"Has there been a change of plans?" Zigor asked.

"What do you mean?"

"Your plan was to have the American businessman and the target deliver the money then you were to persuade the target to admit his guilt and beg for forgiveness."

Nuria realized Kelmen must have filled Zigor in on the operations specifics. She needed an excuse. "There was a change when I learned the target was already here."

"Then you should have stayed with the original plan

and sped up the timetable."

Nuria avoided answering. Instead, she said, "Even more reason for you to send reinforcements. Payback for our soldier, or I should say soldiers."

After a third long silence, Zigor replied, "I can't get someone to you in time. What about your partner, the little man financing your operation?"

"He's just the money man. Besides, he's all talk and I don't trust him to do anything right."

"You're the one who brought him in. If he doesn't step up, you'll have to make do with who you have."

Zigor hung up before Nuria could get another word in.

Nuria immediately dialed another number and the phone went to voice mail.

"Where the fuck are you?" She screamed.

~

CHAPTER 23

Puyol waited to move until the cop drove away and parked his car down the street. When he joined his fellow cops milling around outside the crime scene, Puyol bent down like he was tying his shoe. He glanced up to see the cop separate from the group and walk toward the detective.

Puyol moved quickly past the dumpster and around the back corner of the building. Mack stood inside an alcove with his earphones pulled from his ears. Puyol filled Mack in on his conversation with the cop then said, "We take the side streets back to the house and we do it in double time."

He led Mack around the far side of the park and up a long narrow alley. He kept Mack on the side streets until they came to *Via Augusta.*

"We're far enough away to take the shortest route now." They stayed on the busy *Via Augusta* for the run back up the gradual hill to the safe house.

Concerned Mack was jumpy, Puyol kept his pace steady. Mack quit paying attention to Puyol and fell behind.

Halfway back to the safe house, Mack tried to rationalize why he was incriminated in a murder. Was it to put him on the defensive? Mack thought of the cops showing his picture around the city and what that could mean. He shook the thought from his head and tried to think good thoughts but his mind wouldn't allow it.

His thoughts turned darker as he imagined what Layla was going through. While fighting the bad visuals, his running speed increased.

Realizing negative thoughts would do no good he took control of his mind and concentrated on how to move forward. The first step was to identify the people involved. He thought of the questions needing to be answered in order to find Layla. With a myriad of questions racing through his mind, Mack's speed increased.

He was unaware he was running hard until he passed Puyol as if he were out for a Sunday stroll. He turned off *Via Augusta* and went into a full sprint for the last two hundred meters to the safe house.

Coming to the house, he slowed then walked the last twenty meters. Barely breathing hard, he turned around to see Puyol fifty meters back, slowing to a jog.

As Puyol approached, he said, "At your pace, you'd

have beaten Usain Bolt. I don't know how much running you do in baseball but you, my friend, should have played *fútbol.* We could have used you at Barça."

Mack nodded absentmindedly as his attention was focused elsewhere, on finding Layla.

Kessler and Garcia sat at the kitchen table, both staring at the steam rising from the coffee cups cradled in their hands. They were conversing in hushed voices.

Mack strolled into the kitchen followed closely by Puyol. As soon as Mack and Puyol entered, Kessler and Garcia stopped talking and turned their heads. Garcia blushed and Kessler carried a guilty smile.

Mack didn't need to ask why they had guilt written all over their faces. He walked to the refrigerator, removed two small plastic bottle of water and tossed one to Puyol.

Mack sucked down a long drink from the bottle then made his way to the table.

Puyol plopped down in a chair, took a swig of water and proceeded to tell Kessler and Garcia of his encounter with the cops in *El Raval.* He recounted the murder described by the detective and their search for the two suspects, William McMillan, aka Billy Mack and John Kessler. When he finished, he brought the bottle to his lips, tipped it back and guzzled the entire bottle.

The news didn't seem to faze Kessler. He stared at Mack and said, "Layla was there." There was no doubt in his voice. "And they've moved her."

Mack dropped his eyes then his chin when Kessler confirmed his suspicion.

"Think positive, Billy," Garcia said. "Weary totes a

heavy load. You must be on top of your game."

Kessler added, "Get back that confidence you displayed stepping into the batter's box when you were needed to drive in a run. Hell, in every clutch situation you faced."

Mack sat up and rotated his head, looking everyone squarely in the eye with a firm resolve. Time to step up. He didn't need to say a word.

"Okay good," Garcia said. "We need to determine where Layla was moved and we need to act fast, before we make the ransom drop."

Puyol walked out of the kitchen without saying a word.

Mack took the opportunity to ask, "What's going on with you two?"

Garcia and Kessler looked at each other as if deciding who would answer.

Kessler said, "We had a long-needed talk, worked the kinks out, you might say. We are on the same page now."

Garcia nodded her agreement.

"Kinks, right. If you two resume your personal relationship, that's your business... unless it interferes with finding Layla. That's my one rule."

"Ahhh, the Billy Rule," Garcia said. She gave Mack a serious look. "You can lay that worry to rest. We're professionals. We're here for Layla and that's our only objective, our priority."

Puyol returned with Trinity in his hands. He placed her on the table and opened the screen. "We give Trinity the information we've learned and see what she comes up with. If she's as smart as Caroline says, we utilize every skill she has."

Trinity came on the screen, turned her head left and right and nodded her greetings. Suddenly the background on the screen was an exact duplicate of the kitchen, as if she were sitting at the same table.

"Good morning," Trinity said. "How was your run, Billy, Carles?"

Puyol raised his eyebrows and said, "Does she know everything?"

"What I don't know, I figure out," Trinity answered. "Now, before we start, I have a message from Caroline. She asks that Billy call her after we finish here."

"Let me tell you what we know," Mack said. "Carles spoke with a Barcelona detective about a murder in *El Raval.* The location is an apartment a few blocks from the sea."

Puyol repeated what the detective said.

A black and white headshot of a man in a police uniform popped onto the computer screen.

Trinity said, "The man murdered in *El Raval* last night is Ignacio Ybarra, goes by the nickname, Nacho. He was a police officer in the city of Pamplona until six years ago when he disappeared while investigating the Basque separatist group, *Euskadi Ta Askatasuna*, commonly known as ETA. There is something unusual. His father petitioned to have him declared dead before the normal waiting period when no body is found. He was paid an insurance sum of two hundred and fifty thousand Euros by the city of Pamplona and the Spanish government. The money was withdrawn in cash a day after it hit the father's account. This is the seed money from Pamplona for Xavier Ybarra's apartment rental business.

The headshot of another policeman came on the screen.

"The man pictured here is Xavier Ybarra, the brother of the man murdered in *El Raval.* Xavier died from a seven-story fall. Ignacio Ybarra-"

Mack interrupted, "This is what Layla was trying to tell us when she said the dead cop from Penzance. She knew Ignacio Ybarra, or Nacho, was a cop and for some reason was officially listed as dead."

"Do you think Layla killed Nacho and she wanted us to know?" Kessler asked

"The timing doesn't support your hypothesis." Trinity said. "When Layla gave the Penzance clue, Ignacio was still alive."

Mack added, "She didn't kill the cop in Penzance. The cop's own mother shot him to death."

"That could mean Nacho was killed by someone he knows." Garcia said.

"That means we're back to square one," Kessler said.

Mack turned the computer so he directly faced the screen. "Trinity, have you learned anything about the whereabouts of the kidnappers and Layla and if not, do you have any hunches?"

"J Otis Weil is staying at the Arts Hotel Barcelona in a penthouse suite. I know Mr. Weil is currently inside his suite because he called down to order Bloody Mary mix and a bottle of vodka. Unfortunately, I do not have visual access inside the hotel.

"Since there are few traffic cameras and no security cameras near the locations of either of the Ybarra murders, I do not have any information other than what is in the police reports. The murders occurred in apartments owned by Xavier Ybarra. I have sent you an updated list of all the apartments owned by him. Each of you has it on your phone. The list is broken down by proximity to the apartment in *El Raval* then by occupancy, rented or vacant, and finally, the name on the lease contract."

Billy said, "Let's cut to the chase. What about Layla? Anything on her?" There was disappointment in Mack's voice.

"You asked about the kidnappers first so I started with what I know about them."

"Sorry," Billy answered. "From now on, I'll be more specific."

"I have a traffic cam photo of Layla and a scrawny young man with a tight grip on her arm. Layla is looking up, exposing her face to anyone or anything to see."

"Good girl," Mack said softly.

"The camera is located on the west side of the *La Sagrada Familia.*"

"Scrawny?" Garcia asked. "I have not heard that word before."

"Scrawny means thin to the point of being unhealthy. It is the best definition I could find matching his body type. In the picture, the two were heading west from the Basilica toward the *Gràcia* District. That's in the center of the city. I am reviewing all visual information I can find to determine exactly where they are headed. Luckily, the *Gràcia* District is Barcelona's smallest at four-point-two square kilometers. However, it also the second-most densely populated District in the city with one hundred-twenty thousand inhabitants. The streets are narrow and the buildings are mainly low-rise, as you see."

A video flashed on the screen showing street scenes of narrow roads with cars and mopeds parked on only one side of each street. Old, run-down three and four-story buildings ran along tree-lined streets. In each scene, the sunny sidewalks were crowded.

"I believe the young man is the same person in the photos at Miami International Airport. He boarded the same plane as Layla."

Two photos came on the screen, side-by-side. On the left was the picture of Layla on the tarmac in Miami. On the right was the picture of her and Jordi on a Barcelona street. Jordi had a smirk on his face and a tight grip on her wrist.

"I have run a reliable facial recognition program but I am still unable to come up with a name of the scrawny man. I've determined his height, weight and other measurements. With ninety-nine percent accuracy, I can say the man in the two pictures is the same person. Unfortunately, it may take too long to attach a name, if I get one at all."

Mack stood and stretched. He dropped his palms on the table and said, "After I speak with Caroline, we reconvene here in thirty minutes to prepare for the ransom drop."

"Before you go, I have information you must hear," Trinity said. "The *Guàrdia Urbana* has issued an arrest warrant for both William A. McMillan and John W. Kessler." The arrest warrant with pictures of Mack and

Kessler popped onto the screen. It was the same warrant the cop showed to Puyol.

"We can't worry about that right now," Mack said. "We can deal with it after we find Layla."

Garcia wagged her finger. "We have to deal with it now. We can't afford for you and John to be hauled in."

Trinity cleared her throat and said, "Ray Gunn is on the phone with the mayor of Barcelona as we speak. I'm recording it and will send it to you once the call is completed."

Kessler said, "Maite's right, we avoid the cops. We let Gunn handle the politics and the cops while we focus on the task at hand. We are definitely walking into a set-up and we're still at square one. Maite has an excellent plan but I want everyone to think about what could go sideways at the drop and how we prepare for each contingency."

"I don't like the idea of Billy and you being exposed," Garcia said.

Kessler checked his watch. "We don't have the time to bring in any reinforcements."

"Keep it simple," Garcia said.

"Nothing will happen until we deliver all the money," Mack said. "Keep that in mind."

Garcia strummed her fingers rhythmically on the table. "Billy, don't assume anything. We have amateurs mixed in with pros and that's a recipe for disaster."

Mack fished his phone from his pocket and meandered outside to call Caroline.

~

CHAPTER 24

J Otis listened to Nuria's screeching voice mail and rolled his eyes as the limo cruised past Camp Nou, the large soccer stadium on the western side of the city.

The long street was lined with identical large white concrete buildings housing small apartments and even smaller balconies, all with identical wrought iron railings. Dark green shades were pulled down and attached to the railings to block the sun. Jutting out from each balcony was the same small gray satellite dish. It was as if one architect used only one set of blueprints.

How can people live like this? Get a life. J Otis thought. He shook his loathing from his mind. He had a real problem. The ransom was about to be paid and he hadn't heard back from Arkady or Vlad.

The limo turned onto a side street that was devoid of streetlights. The limo slowed to a stop in front of the new hideout - the smallest building on the street.

There was only one functioning apartment in the building and it needed work. There was a garage but it was too small for a limousine. J Otis eyed the hideaway and corrected himself. The hideaway was merely a weekly rental apartment, a typical place where the wretched poor scraped together just enough money to rent for a week's vacation. It disgusted J Otis to have to walk into a place like this. It was beneath him. Layla will be happy when she arrived in Moscow and to a house in which people wanted to live.

J Otis shook his head as he stepped out of the limo. He loathed poor people, always wanting, begging. He reluctantly strolled to the front door willing his phone to ring. He paused at the door and checked his phone pleading for it to show a missed call from Arkady.

Nothing.

He pushed open the door. Nuria stood in the middle of the room holding a lit cigarette in one hand and a glass of whiskey in the other.

"I have good news," Nuria said. "Jordi called and we had a good talk. He's bringing the little bitch back to me."

"When?"

"He'll be here soon."

"I'll believe it when I see the girl," J Otis replied as he studied his phone begging for it to ring.

Nuria dropped her cigarette on the floor and smothered it with her foot. She grinned widely then said, "If you doubt my son again I will give him Layla."

Keeping an eye on J Otis, she placed her drink down. She said, "I'll be right back," and hurried out the door before he could respond.

Nuria marched down the street and took the first left. In the middle of the block, she stopped, checked to see if she was followed then strolled into a small restaurant.

Running along the wall to the right was a long stainless steel counter with a selection of *tapas* behind a curved glass countertop. Resting on top of the glass were small plates filled with the same *tapas* from directly below. The bright fluorescent lights hurt her eyes causing her to blink repeatedly.

Nuria grabbed a plate of thinly sliced ham and ordered a whiskey with no ice from the woman standing behind the glass case.

Kelmen sat in the back corner facing the front door. There was an empty plate and an empty beer glass sitting on the table in front of him. He had a commonplace look to him. His only distinguishing feature was his lightly tanned skin. He was a perfect operative: nondescript, someone you would walk past without noticing. He was also the top assassin for ETA.

Nuria set her plate down and stared at the woman behind the counter until she brought Nuria her glass of whiskey.

"Good morning," the waitress said in Catalan and set the glass of Whiskey in front of Nuria.

As soon as the waitress left, Nuria said, "Your cleaner did an adequate job. Thank him for me."

"Thank him by paying him what we agreed."

“It’ll be taken care of it. With his help, we're back on track. I'll have the girl in time for the ransom drop and I'm confident the Russian will take my deal."

Kelmen sat back. "So, you don't need me to kill Billy Mack and take Kessler anymore? Weil agreed to step up and replace Nacho?"

"I only need you to grab Kessler. If you have to kill Billy Mack I'm not paying for it.” Nuria took a swig of her whiskey then licked her lips. “The answer to your second question is no, J Otis is incapable of stepping up."

"What about the Russians?"

"There is only one Russian, a thug named Vlad. I called his father in Moscow and offered him half of J Otis' share if his son kills J Otis... after I have Kessler, of course. The father promised to get back to me."

"And Billy Mack?"

"I don't give a fuck about him. He's J Otis' problem."

Kelmen waved the waitress over and ordered another beer. When she was out of earshot, he said, "Our boss wants Kessler alive when you bring him to Pamplona."

"Tell Zigor that Kessler will be alive... barely."

"Let me give you a little piece of advice," Kelmen said and waited for Nuria to look him in the eye. "Bring Kessler directly to Zigor. He has two dead sons. The deaths are fresh and he is hurting."

Nuria held her breath then exhaled slowly before downing her glass of whiskey. She said, "You don't think I'm grieving? I lost my daughter and husband when Kessler executed them in cold blood."

Nuria finished her whiskey and lit a cigarette. In the

mirror behind Kelmen, she saw the waitress take a step toward her waving her finger no.

Nuria turned and glared at her with a death stare then shook her head. The waitress turned and walked back behind the counter.

Kelmen said, "Bringing Kessler directly to Zigor shows your respect for our leader. He will extract his revenge then give Kessler back to you so you can extract what the murderer deserves then kill him."

Nuria dropped her cigarette into her empty glass then spit into the glass to put the cigarette out. "If Zigor wants Kessler first, he has to come to Barcelona to extract his revenge. After I kill that asshole, I plan to drive his battered, dead body to Madrid and drop it in the parking lot in *San Sebastián de los Reyes*, where my daughter and husband were executed. It will be a warning to the world and to every Spaniard to give us back our country. Then I will die the hero of my people."

"Zigor may not leave Pamplona until his two sons are buried. He's on edge and if you defy him, you won't live to regret it."

"My source inside the *Guardia* tells me that given the circumstances of Nacho's fake death, Zigor has some explaining to do in person or they won't release the body. Besides, I don't really give a damn what happens to me. He would only be taking a month or two away from me."

Kelmen leaned forward, "Either way, you do what Zigor demands. Remember, you have a son, a mentally disturbed son. If Zigor doesn't get what he wants, he will exact his revenge on you by killing Jordi in front of you before he kills you."

Nuria lit another cigarette. "Fine, but then tell Zigor I want assurances Jordi will be taken care for the rest of his life."

"No one *tells* Zigor what to do."

~

Jordi crept into the studio apartment hoping to find Layla asleep on her back. He wanted to crawl on top of her before she could react. He peeked over at the bed.

Layla sat with her back against the wall and her knees pulled tightly to her chest. She glared at Jordi.

Jordi cautiously approached the bed. When he saw the look in Layla's eyes, he moved away then walked around the room picking up her clothes.

He brought the clothes over to the bed and threw them at her. "Get dressed, we're leaving," he ordered.

Before Layla could grab her panties, Jordi snatched them off the mattress and brought them to his nose. He sucked in a deep breath and then exhaled slowly. "*Mmmmmm.*"

Layla turned her head away. She couldn't look at him.

"I'm keeping these," he said. He shoved the panties inside his pants and massaged himself. "*Ahhhhhh.*"

~

CHAPTER 25

A vigorous pounding on the apartment door startled J Otis. With Nuria gone, he didn't expect any visitors, at least none who would knock. He glided over to the window and peeked out the corner of the pulled-down shade.

Vlad stood in the doorway, dressed in all black, his hair pulled back into a tight ponytail and his black briefcase in his right hand. Vlad looked over at J Otis and grinned mischievously. "Open up," he yelled.

J Otis pulled open the door and stepped aside.

Vlad strutted in and placed the briefcase on the floor in middle of the room. He opened the case and removed a Browning 1911-380 from its custom foam padding. The black and silver pistol had a custom, combat grip and a six-inch barrel with laser sight attached. He held it up for J Otis to see.

"This is the most accurate handgun in the world. I could shoot off a fly's dick at fifty meters. That's how good I am with this piece." He pointed the gun at J Otis and a red dot danced on J Otis' chest. "So... where do you want it? Heart? Head? Eyes?"

J Otis' legs nearly gave out. He grabbed the back of a chair as he struggled to breathe.

Vlad broke out into a hearty laugh. When he caught his breath he said, "I love seeing the reaction on a man's face when I do that." He immediately stopped laughing and said, "I find it funny that nobody ever answers me," then laughed uncontrollably.

J Otis plopped down into the chair, unable to speak.

Vlad sat across from J Otis, a wide grin stuck on his face. He said, "I spoke with my father. He wants me to pass on a message. He will agree to your terms if you give me your partner's share, the one-and-a-half million plus a bonus of five-hundred thousand."

J Otis could only nod his head up and down. After a number of deep breaths, he finally said, "Agreed." His voice was weak, raspy.

"Good, my father does not want you to call him anymore. He thinks your phone is bugged. You can see him when we are back in Moscow." Vlad walked over to his briefcase and placed the Browning back in its place.

J Otis heard a commotion outside the door. He jumped up and swiftly moved behind the chair.

Vlad snatched the Browning from the foam padding and aimed it at the front door.

Nuria threw open the door and stepped inside.

A red laser dot hit her forehead.

"Don't Vlad," J Otis yelled.

Vlad dropped his hand and glared at Nuria.

"You're lucky Vlad didn't kill you," J Otis said.

"Fuck you, J Otis." Nuria marched past Vlad and J Otis and into the kitchen.

J Otis heard the clink of glass then the scuffling of feet.

Nuria appeared in the doorway with a glass of whiskey in her hand and a cigarette between her lips.

"I have great news. Jordi is on his way back with the little bitch and she will be available when Mack or Kessler demand to talk to her."

J Otis checked at the clock on the wall. "When is she getting here?"

"She gets here when she gets here. Go upstairs and get her room ready?"

"That's your job."

"Look J Otis, if I'm not down here when they get here, Jordi may take off. He's fragile right now."

"He's a retard," J Otis mumbled under his breath as he climbed the stairs.

Nuria strolled over to the steps and watched J Otis enter Layla's new room. Confident he couldn't hear her she walked over to Vlad.

"I spoke with your father. He's agreed to my terms."

"You mean you agreed to his terms."

"Whatever. When I get Kessler, you get your money and you can kill Mack and J Otis if you want. I don't give a shit either way. Kessler is all I want. Once I get Kessler, you get your bonus."

"I like what I hear."

Nuria's phone rang. She pulled it out of her back pocket and brought it to her ear.

"Where are you?" she asked.

"I think we are close, mother. What is the address?"

Nuria gave Jordi the address and a description of the building. She hung up and walked to the door.

She opened the door hoping not to startle Jordi. There was no one outside so she stepped out onto the walkway. Down the street, Jordi had his left arm tightly around Layla's shoulder and his right hand cupping her breast.

Every few steps, Layla would stop walking and Jordi would drag her a few feet. When she fought, he pulled her up and said something to get her walking again.

As Jordi walked up to the apartment, he said, "See mother, I told you I didn't hurt her."

When he reached the door, Nuria jerked Layla away from Jordi and pushed her into the house. She yanked her across the floor and shoved her down into a chair.

She turned to Vlad. "Take her upstairs to the top floor and make sure she's secured to the bed."

Vlad took Layla by the arm and led her to the stairs.

When Vlad and Layla were halfway up the stairs, Nuria said, "Don't let J Otis be alone with her."

"I won't."

"You don't touch her either, got that?"

"Don't worry, I don't touch kids."

Nuria turned back to Jordi.

He smiled up at her, proud of bringing Layla back. "I

did good. Now we can get the bastard man who killed father and sister."

Nuria wanted to slap him but held her hand steady. She had to get through to him. She needed him to guard Layla while her team was getting Kessler and the money.

"I have to go get the bastard man who killed father and sister and I need you to do exactly what I'm about to tell you while I am gone. Do not touch the girl or even talk to her. She is evil and will make bad things happen to you if you touch her before we kill Kessler."

"But what if she *wants* to play? She is always looking at me like she wants to."

"If you don't touch her or talk to her while I'm gone, I will let you play with her as much as you want when I get back. Do you understand?"

"Yes, mother," Jordi replied, practically drooling as he answered.

~

CHAPTER 26

Outside the safe house, Mack moved away from the door and was about to tap Caroline's number into his phone when it rang. He perused the street for any cop cars, marked or unmarked. Seeing nothing suspicious, he looked up at the morning sky. Dark clouds were on the western horizon. He hoped it wasn't a harbinger of things to come. A Vespa zipped by on the one-way street. The harsh shrill of its two-stroke motor hurt Mack's ears.

He recognized the number, brought the phone to his right ear and stuck his finger in his other ear so he could hear.

"Hello Billy," Caroline said, a little too cheery for Mack.

"Trinity said you wanted to talk with me." Mack

replied.

"Trinity never lies. She doesn't know how. I want to update you on what's in place and what I've learned."

"I'm all ears."

The same Vespa zoomed by from the other direction. The driver had a bad-boy smile on his face because he was going down the wrong way.

"Go back inside and put the phone on speaker so everyone can hear." Caroline yelled.

"How did you-?" Mack caught himself and strolled inside. He made his way to the kitchen to find Garcia and Kessler still sitting at the table. Puyol stood at the counter pouring a cup of coffee.

Mack tapped the speaker button and set his phone on the table. He reached over, rotated Trinity on the table and pointed the screen towards the phone.

"Everyone is here, Caroline."

"I know your time is short so I'll be brief and just give the relevant points. If you have questions, wait until I finish before you ask. I'll give you the particulars in a second. First off, Ray Gunn had a long conversation with the mayor. She is looking into the murders and will get back to Gunn as soon as she knows something. She's a politician so you can't expect anything useful. You should assume you're on your own for the time being. Stay away from law enforcement." The sound of papers being shuffled ruffled through the speaker. "That being said, neither Nimesh nor I were able to hack the GPS on the satellite phone used for the ransom call but, as Trinity informed you, we installed a cutting-edge eavesdropping program on that phone. Trinity has recordings of all conversations for you to hear. There isn't a whole lot of useful information providing the whereabouts of Layla but I can tell you one thing. This is set up. Billy, there is a hit ordered on you, but the woman, to use her words, 'doesn't give a shit if you're killed or not.

"Her sole focus is on you, John. You are to be taken alive but your fate is worse than death. The woman's name is either Nuria or Neria. I heard both on the recordings. She met a man in a restaurant and was ordered to deliver you to the head of the military wing of ETA. The man in the restaurant is probably a pro but I haven't yet identified him. I'm working my sources to get a name but my gut tells me he's somehow tied to the man murdered in *El Raval*, to the cop who swan dived out his window and to the ETA leader.

"That being said, there are two pros working with Nuria or Neria and J Otis Weil. The man in the restaurant is Basque and I know this because he speaks Basque with the woman. The other pro is Eastern European. Russian is my guess. He speaks decent English but with an accent. I can only surmise they are in Barcelona to kill Billy and take John. Be very careful when you make the exchange.

"Nimesh and I will monitor the situation. He just arrived in Einsiedeln and has set up his team. I have also been authorized to inform you Ray Gunn is here leading our efforts.

"Finally, Jordi, the son of the woman named Nuria or Neria, is more than a few demented bricks short. He has Layla and is bringing her back to his mother. I don't have any information relating to why he took Layla, where he had her or why he is now bringing her back.

Now you are up-to-date with what I know. Are there any questions?"

Garcia raised her hand quickly, stopping anyone from asking a question. "Did you say Neria, spelled N-E-R-I-A?"

"Yes, that name slipped out during a conversation with the boss in Pamplona."

Garcia slowly gazed around the room then said, "That has to be Neria Otxoa, the notorious ETA terrorist wanted in Spain and France for multiple killings. Ever since her husband and daughter died at my hands, she's been on a killing spree targeting Spanish officials. If civilians got in the way, she killed them too."

The picture of a younger, chubby Neria Otxoa flashed on the full screen then shrunk down to the left corner. "This picture is from an old national identity card for Neria Otxoa," Trinity said.

A grainy picture of a skinny young boy filled the screen then shrunk down to the right corner.

"That's the kid in the pictures from Miami and near La Sagrada Familia," Mack said, pointing at the picture.

Trinity said, "That is Jordi Otxoa. He's eighteen years old... physically."

"The boy is mentally disturbed and that's putting it mildly," Caroline added. She cleared her throat as if she didn't want to say what was coming next. "We have a thin file on him because he's so young. We know he's a psychopath. He's amoral, antisocial, unable to distinguish right from wrong, doesn't know how to relate to people and, in this kid's case, extremely violent if he doesn't get his way."

"Why was he alone with Layla?" Mack asked.

"I can't answer that," Caroline said.

Mack closed his eyes and clenched his jaw. The air in the room grew stiff, strained.

Mack opened his eyes. "If that sick little deviant touched Layla, I'll kill him. That's *the* Billy Rule!"

Garcia placed her hand on Mack's arm. "I have just the weapon for you upstairs in my room. It'll more than do the job. But, wait to kill the little deviant until we have Layla. She's what matters."

Nimesh's voice came over the speaker. "Although I was able to lock onto J Otis Weil's phone with a GPS tracker, it won't do much good. That phone has been sitting in the Arts Hotel Barcelona since he arrived. J Otis is using a burner phone. We will continue to monitor and relay all real time information to Trinity, so you will have it when we have it. It will take some time to identify J Otis' burner because we have to track all unregistered phones in Barcelona with voice recognition hoping to zero in on the phone J Otis is using."

"This is Ray Gunn." An authoritative voice boomed through the speaker.

At the recognition of Gunn's voice, Mack, Kessler and Garcia sat up straighter, as if at attention. Puyol smiled at their reaction.

"I have arranged for a satellite to be in position to monitor the drop at the baseball stadium as well as the location of J Otis' limo, if he uses it. Trinity will assure the information gets to you in real time."

"Is there any way to scan the city, review street cam footage to try and recognize Layla or anyone else?" Mack asked.

"The technology exists but with the ransom drop only an hour or so away, it can't be done in time," Trinity answered.

"Even if we narrow the search to locations near the apartments owned by Xavier Ybarra?" Mack asked.

"It will cut down my search time but the window may still be too short."

"Do it anyway, it can't hurt."

"It's already running," Gunn added. "Now, listen closely. It's obvious now the drop is a set-up. It is payback for the op that killed Jordi Otxoa, his daughter and his nephew. The Otxoa's are convinced Kessler executed them in cold blood. Our intel inside Spain confirms that. A reliable source has evidence indicating the top hitter for ETA is involved. Neria Otxoa is too high ranking in ETA not to muster the top resources of that organization."

Garcia leaned toward the phone. "Why is Billy Mack involved? He had no connection to the Otxoa op."

"His connection is to me," Gunn replied. "Somehow someone was able to connect Kessler to me and then to Billy. That somebody had to be J Otis Weil. How J Otis is connected with the Otxoa family is a mystery."

"But there was no Ray Gunn involved in the Otxoa op." Kessler said.

"I know and I have people digging into this," Gunn replied. "If there is a leak, I will find it and plug it, permanently."

Puyol pushed his chair from the table and stood. "The leak most likely didn't come from Spain. No one here knows a Ray Gunn. Let me work with Nimesh to flush this out."

"We can worry about that after Layla is safe and sound," Mack said. "It's time to get ready for the drop."

~

CHAPTER 27

Thirty minutes later, Mack came down the steps ready for the ransom drop. He was the first one ready and carried the two duffel bags stuffed with money to the front door. He dropped the bags with a thud and checked his phone for any messages from Trinity.

A minute later, Garcia walked in with an attaché in her hand. She laid it on the floor, popped it open and removed a large handgun with a black grip, silver cylinder and long, silver barrel.

"Have you ever seen Dirty Harry?"

Mack nodded, "Who hasn't?"

Garcia held up the gun. "This is a Smith & Wesson 500, a fifty-caliber handgun that makes Dirty Harry's .44 Magnum look like a Saturday night special. You hit that little pervert with this and the only thing left of him will be his demented smile." Garcia grinned at her joke. "It's double action so there will be a kick to it. Think you can handle it?"

Mack held out his hand.

Garcia handed him the gun handle up, barrel down.

When Garcia released her grip on the gun Mack's arm dropped a couple inches.

"Heavy," he said.

"It's easily controllable but, as with any gun, it depends on your aim."

"I hope I won't need to use it."

"*Yo tambien*," Garcia said then reached down to the attaché, lifted out a custom leather back holster and handed it to Mack.

"Me Too," she repeated in English.

Mack admired the holster's leather craftwork.

"This will make it easy to carry and help conceal it. Are you right handed?"

"I throw right-handed and bat left-handed," Mack said. He took off his sport coat and lifted his black t-shirt.

Garcia situated the holster in the small of his back, inside his khakis.

Garcia double-checked the holster and slid the handgun in place. "Work on drawing the gun. Get used to the feel."

Puyol strolled into the foyer dressed casually, like a tourist going out for a nice lunch. "The car is out front. I will drive until we reach *Montjuic*. That's where Maite, and I get out. It will take a little time to get in position so stay in the car until you hear from us. That will be Billy's cue to walk out to the spot ordered by the kidnappers." Puyol waited until Mack placed the gun back in its holster.

"They will have eyes on you Billy and you can be sure they will be upset you don't have all the money with you."

"That's the idea, knock them off-balance. They won't kill me until they get the money."

Puyol saw the bulge from the large handgun holstered to Mack's back. "Don't bring that cannon with you when you walk to the spot. If the bad guys see that bulge in your back, they'll pump you full of holes. Leave it in the car. You won't need it until we go get Layla."

"What if she's there and so is the kid?"

"Neither of them will be there. That's not how kidnappings go down. You'll get a call demanding you get the money as instructed. When they see Kessler bringing the money, they will give you further instructions."

Kessler walked into the foyer wearing jeans and his college football jersey. "If I'm goin' down, I'm goin' down in style." He smiled at Mack. "Just kidding, this is my lucky jersey. I wore it when we won the national championship."

Garcia rolled her eyes. "I hate that jersey." She eyed him up and down then cocked her head. "At least it still fits."

"*Ens n'anem*," Puyol said in Catalan.

Mack glanced over at Garcia.

"Let's go," she translated.

Mack's phone beeped, he had a message. He tapped the phone and Trinity's voice came over the speaker. "Here is the most recent recording concerning Layla."

She played the recording. Nuria's voice came on followed by the voice of what sounded like a young boy.

Everyone huddled around the phone. When the conversation ended, Mack said, "They are not going to let Layla go. These people are sick."

"All the more reason to demand to speak with Layla before we hand over any money," Kessler said.

"Kessler cannot show his face until Mack hears Layla voice and is certain she's alive. Then we need to slow roll them." Puyol added.

Trinity's voice came over Mack's phone. "I have all my programs in hyper-drive mode. Be sure to keep your phones on vibrate at all times."

Kessler removed a handgun from his waistband holster and readied it.

"What kind of gun is that?" Mack asked. The pistol had a stainless steel frame and wood grips with multiple scratches. "I've never seen a grip like that."

""This is a Tanfoglio Mossad 9 millimeter. It was a gift from a *friend.* An Israeli agent and I were in a firefight with Hezbollah in Lebanon. I saved her life and she gave me this as a gift."

Garcia pursed her lips and shook her head. She didn't want to hear the story again.

While Kessler slid his gun back into its holster, Puyol lifted both duffel bags full of money and carried them to the door. He tapped in the security code on his phone and the door eased open.

Waiting on the curb with the motor running was a black cargo van with its windows blacked out, including the windshield.

Puyol threw the duffel bags in the back and tossed the keys to Kessler. "I changed my mind. You drive, I'll navigate."

The drive to *Montjuic* and the Olympic grounds was slow. Inside the van, there was a nervous silence.

The Olympic grounds came into view up above them. The white curvy, futuristic Olympic ring and high diving platform stood out. Mack remembered watching the Olympic diving competition on TV. As the divers flipped, turned and twisted, Mack's attention kept getting diverted to *La Sagrada Familia* in the distant background. He tried to remember if any Olympic baseball games were televised.

The van slowed as Puyol gave Kessler evasive maneuver instructions in case they were being followed.

At the base of *Montjuic*, Kessler pulled the van to the curb and killed the motor. He looked at his watch. "It's go time. Let's do this," he said.

Garcia handed out flesh-colored ear buds and everyone inserted them in their ear. She handed out what looked like a small round, flesh colored band-aid. "This is your microphone, stick it behind your ear. Only speak when absolutely necessary."

Garcia strapped her holster to her thigh, attached the silencer to her pistol and slid in her piece.

Garcia and Puyol hopped out of the van and disappeared behind the hedges separating the road from the walking path leading up to the Olympic venues atop *Montjuic*.

Kessler started the engine, pulled the van back on

the street and cruised up the single lane road. He said, "Maite gave me a back way in, just in case. From there, you can make it to the drop site without being seen. So will I."

Mack stared out the window thinking of Layla.

The van approached the baseball stadium from right field. Kessler drove around the outfield and parked the van inside a thick clump of trees a stone's throw from the left field fence.

Mack stepped out of the van then handed Kessler his Smith & Wesson 500. "See you on the pitcher's mound."

"*Vaya con Dios.*"

~

CHAPTER 28

J Otis and Vlad came down from Layla's room grinning. Vlad carried his Browning in his right hand like it was a natural extension.

"I had a talk with Layla," J Otis said. "She knows what she is to say and nothing more. Vlad made it painfully obvious what will happen if she doesn't do exactly as we say. There won't be a repeat of the last call."

Vlad aimed his pistol at Jordi, the laser sight drilling into the boy's forehead. He said, "I like that girl, she's feisty. Nobody touches her while I'm gone. I'm talking to you kid."

Jordi was paying Vlad no attention. He rocked back and forth staring up at nothing in particular.

Nuria strolled over and stroked Jordi's hair. She took

him by the hand and led him into the kitchen. She hugged him and whispered in his ear, "If I don't come back in three hours, you take the girl to the hiding place. If you don't touch her until it gets dark, you can play with her all you want when you are hiding. When you get to the hiding place call Uncle Zigor and have him come get you, both of you."

"You aren't coming back mother?"

Nuria kissed him firmly on the lips then petted him on the top of his head. "It is just like I told you many times before. If mother has an accident, you must do what I've told you."

Nuria marched into the living area. "I had a talk with him," she said. "He understands the little bitch is to be left alone until we get back."

Jordi crept into the room, slinked over to the chair by the window and sat down. He resumed rocking back and forth, smiling blankly.

"I think it best I stay here while you and Vlad get the ransom money," J Otis said.

Nuria lit a cigarette. She wasn't about to let J Otis be alone with Jordi or the girl. "No, we all leave for the drop now." She handed a burner phone to Jordi and an index card with a short script on the front in blue ink and another short script on the back in red ink.

"At exactly twelve o'clock, call Billy Mack by pressing the green button on the phone. When he answers, read the words written in blue then let him speak with Layla." Nuria turned the card over. "She must only read the words in red. Make sure she doesn't say anything else. As soon as she finishes reading these words, you hang up.

You understand?"

Jordi repeatedly flipped the card over and back. He smiled up at his mother. "What if she wants to play with me?"

Nuria leaned down, her face close to Jordi's. "Remember what mother said, that girl is evil. She doesn't want to play with you. She is trying to trick you so she can hurt you. Mother doesn't want you to get hurt."

A confused look washed over Jordi's face.

Nuria whispered in Jordi's ear, "If you don't do exactly as mother instructed, mother will get hurt and you will never see her again. You must make the call at twelve o'clock and do exactly as I said. Never forget that I am the only one who loves you."

"I won't forget."

Nuria grabbed her satellite phone and marched to the door. She waited for J Otis and Vlad to walk out then turned back to Jordi and said. "If you're good, I will bring you back an ice cream."

Walking to the street, Nuria looked around then asked, "Where's the limo?"

"Vlad was resourceful and got us a new vehicle. It won't draw attention to us."

At the curb was a gray Renault Kangoo van. A small workman's vehicle with its back windows covered.

J Otis opened the back door and jumped in. There was only a single bucket seat in the back. "Nuria, you sit up front with Vlad."

Nuria sat in the front passenger's seat and lit a cigarette.

Vlad started the engine, checked the side mirror then

pulled out into the street.

Fifty meters down the street, J Otis said, "Your kid better not fuck up. If he does, you're putting Vlad and me in danger. I don't have to tell you what that means."

"Fuck you, J Otis. Jordi will do me proud."

"I don't want to hear another word from either of you until we get to the rendezvous point, got that," Vlad said and held up his Browning for emphasis.

~

At a concrete parking ramp across from the baseball stadium, Vlad drove up to the third level and parked the van against the wall overlooking the stadium. From their perch, they could look down on the field.

Nuria looked above the field to a spot in the press box to see if Kelmen was in place. She was hoping to at least catch a glimpse of him, giving her reassurance. Kelmen was the ultimate professional so odds were he would be invisible.

Vlad spotted Mack walking the fence line. He was carrying only one Adidas bag.

"Only one of them is showing up," Vlad said. "Based on size, I say is Billy Mack. Where is big man, Kessler?"

Nuria whipped her head around. A sharp pain shot through her neck. She grabbed the back of her neck and massaged the pain. She stared icily at the field, seeing only Billy Mack. "Where the fuck is the murderer?"

J Otis pounded his fist. "Where the fuck is the other half of my money?"

~

Jordi looked up at the clock on the wall. He had a few minutes before he made the call for mother. He crept up the stairs with the phone in one hand and the index card in the other. At the door, he leered at Layla lying half-naked on the bed. She turned away from him.

He tiptoed to the bed.

"After you talk on the telephone, we can play. Mother said it was okay." Jordi put one knee on the bed.

Layla felt his weight on the bed but didn't move. She said, "Your mother ordered you not to play with me. If you disobey her, I will tell her, then she will leave you and you will be all alone." Layla hoped that would scare him.

It didn't.

Jordi put his other knee on the bed. "After you talk on the phone, mother said we can play together."

Jordi flipped the card back and forth a number of times then laid down next to Layla and held up the card. "When I give you the phone, you must only say what is written in red."

~

CHAPTER 29

Mack hugged the tree line running along the street until he was fifty feet from the third base dugout. He marched through the open ground to the fence line. With both hands, he tossed the duffel bag over the short fence, hopped over and walked onto the field. As he crossed the third base line, he looked down to see a red laser dot hitting the center of his chest.

He slowed his pace as he approached the pitchers mound. As soon as he stood on top of the mound, he dropped the duffel bag. A second later, his phone rang. He slowly lifted it to his ear.

"Where's Kessler and where's the money, dead man?" The woman's voice was shrill, angry.

Mack assumed the caller was Neria Otxoa. "I told

you I wouldn't hand over the money or Kessler until I talked to Layla and was satisfied she wasn't hurt, abused or even touched by you or your mentally disturbed kid."

A sharp laugh came through the phone followed by an intense coughing fit. When the coughing subsided, she said, "I’m not the one you should worry about. Now, go get Kessler and the money or you and the girl are both dead."

"Kessler will bring the rest of the money once I talk with Layla. If I don't hear her voice and ask her my questions, no Kessler, no money."

"You see that red dot on your chest? All I have to do is give the order and you're dead. The last thing you'll feel is a horrifying pain then nothing. Then I'm coming over to carve your heart out so I can give it to your little bitch before I kill her."

Mack sucked in a deep breath. This woman was crazy but he had to assume she was bluffing. "I will give up my life if it means saving Layla. If you kill me, you don't get Kessler. That's what this is all about, isn't it?"

Mack listened to Neria's coughing fit for over a minute. When it stopped, he said, "No Layla, no Kessler."

"Wait for the call. You will talk to her in two minutes."

"I'm not going anywhere."

"Good, look around because that's where you're going to die."

Two minutes later, Mack's phone rang. The caller ID read: UNKNOWN.

"Layla?"

"This is Layla's boyfriend, we play together."

"Put Layla on the phone."

"You are to leave the money on the pitchers mound then lie flat on the ground." The person speaking was now obviously reading what he was saying. "Once the money is picked up, you will receive another call telling you where to find... my girlfriend."

"Put Layla on the phone."

Mack heard a sniffling on the phone. "Layla?"

"Billy, it's me. I have to read this." Layla sniffed. "Once the money is collected, you will go to Sants train station and wait for a call giving you my location."

"Are you okay, Layla? Did anyone hurt you? You can tell me the truth."

"It's not like Penzance anymore. The policeman is dead-"

The connection went dead.

The red laser dot was now centered on his heart. He thought about running but that would be suicide. Over past third base, he saw Kessler throw the other bag of money over the fence then easily hop over. He walked casually to the pitchers mound and dropped the money next to the other bag. He saw the confusion on Mack's face.

Trinity patched through your call to all our phones. Let's get this over with."

"I don't see Maite or Carles," Mack said.

"You're not supposed to. If you see either of them, we're dead."

Out of the corner of his eye, Mack saw something

move. Coming out from behind the third base dugout was a man roughly the same size as Kessler. He was dressed in all black and his black hair was pulled back tight, into a ponytail. With the exception of the large pistol hanging from his right hand, he had the same expression on his face as a manager walking out to the mound to change pitchers – stone cold.

As he neared, his expression changed to a smirk and he slowed to an overly cautious pace.

He pointed his Browning at Mack. "You stay here and await further instructions."

He shifted his aim to Kessler. "Pick up bags and we go back the way you come. Once we outside this place, you follow my instructions."

"Who am I talking to?" Kessler asked.

"You can call me Vlad, as in Vlad the Impaler." This time Vlad didn't laugh.

Kessler tried to slow down the ransom payment. "I'm not going with you or giving you the money until I talk to Layla. I want to hear directly from her, assuring me she's alive."

Vlad lifted his Browning and shot Kessler in the leg, nicking his thigh.

Blood gushed out, soaking his pant leg.

Kessler didn't flinch.

"I can't kill you, Mr. Kessler but your friend is fair game." Vlad pointed his gun at Mack chest.

Kessler bent down and picked up the duffel bags. "Let's go."

Kessler dropped one bag as if it were too heavy. He bent down to pick it up and said to Mack, "Maite called an audible."

When Kessler reached the dugout, Mack looked down. The laser dot was gone from his chest. When he looked back up, Kessler was outside the fence carrying both bags. Vlad walked a few meters behind him, aiming his pistol at Kessler's back.

When Kessler and Vlad disappeared inside a concrete parking structure, Mack looked down searching for the red laser dot. He didn't see one so he gingerly stepped off the mound. He quickened his pace to the third base dugout, sat and calmed his breathing.

Garcia came out of the press box high above homeplate and made her way down the steps. She was typing into her phone as she came to the dugout. The silencer attached to her handgun stuck out through the bottom of her holster and ran halfway down her thigh.

"Where's John?" she asked.

"He was escorted out by the man calling himself Vlad. I believe Caroline identified him as Russian. He shot John in the leg."

"Did he walk out?"

"Without a limp."

"John's been shot so many times, he doesn't even feel it any more."

"We have to follow him," Mack said. "Where's Carles?"

"He's on the phone with Gunn. They have two locations identified with a high probability of Layla being at one of them."

"We don't have time to waste. We can't lose Kessler or he's a dead man."

"Don't worry," Garcia said casually. "I have it covered."

Confused by Garcia's casualness, Mack asked, "Aren't you worried?"

"Relax Billy, if you stress out, you make mistakes. John and I are always prepared for the worst. That's why we make a great team. That and one other thing."

"When I arrived, there was a red laser pointed at my chest until John and the Russian left." Mack patted his chest. "Then it went away. What happened to it?"

"The person aiming the laser at you was about to take you out. Fortunately for you, he didn't see me coming."

~

CHAPTER 30

Mack looked out over the grass baseball field, a place where no one should die. Growing up, the baseball field was a refuge for Mack, a safe place to play, compete. His only worry was whether his team won or lost.

Today, he'd almost lost more than a game of baseball on this field.

It took Mack a few seconds to internalize this. "What did you mean when you said, *he didn't see me coming*?"

Garcia studied the screen on her phone before she slid it into her pocket. "Professional killers know if they want a successful hit they can't be completely unseen. In this case, he used a laser sight. I can only assume he didn't think you'd have someone like me on your team. Big mistake."

"How did you know he was there?"

"I saw the laser hitting your chest and followed it back. There was only one place he could be. His focus was on you, waiting. I came up from behind and decided I liked you more than him."

"How can you be so casual about killing a man?"

Garcia's face grew dark, her eyes blinked rapidly. "I never take killing casually." She pulled her phone from her pocket and showed Mack the screen. On it was an Interpol wanted poster. "This is Kel Mendoza, he is known simply as Kelmen. He is a member of ETA and is their best assassin. He also freelances and is paid handsomely. Somebody, not ETA, wants you dead."

"Do you think that's why Layla was taken?"

"That's a small part of the reason. J Otis Weil wants his money back and to kill you for taking it. The bigger reason was to get Kessler. Neria Otxoa wants to exact her revenge on him and for some reason she's desperate."

"That tells me they have no intention of letting Layla go."

“Otxoa doesn’t leave witnesses.”

Mack didn’t know what to say.

Garcia put her hand on Mack’s shoulder for comfort. "Now you know why we were so adamant you talk with Layla throughout the drop. We had to keep her in Barcelona to have a chance of getting her back."

"J Otis has his money and Neria Otxoa has Kessler," Mack said. "We don't have much time. We need to find Layla and Kessler, and fast."

"Give me your phone," Garcia said, holding out her hand.

Mack handed over his phone. Garcia's pointer finger rapidly tapped the screen multiple times. She handed the phone back to Mack.

"Now, both of us are tracking Kessler. So is Trinity."

"Are we tracking his phone?"

"No, John and I have implants under our arms. They are undetectable. Unfortunately, they are short range and can only be traced within a hundred square mile area. That's what makes them undetectable."

"Why didn't you say anything sooner?"

"Would it have mattered?"

Mack's shook his head and lifted his phone. A red dot was slowly moving across the screen. "They are heading west, probably to the airport."

Garcia placed her thumb and index fingers on Mack's screen then slowly separated them. The map zoomed in to where Mack could read the street names.

"They are heading northwest," Garcia said. "I've asked Trinity to triangulate Kessler's implant, if possible, with Otxoa's satellite phone and J Otis's burn phone. Gunn has re-routed a satellite to over the city, tracking John. When John stops moving, we start moving and fast."

"Where's Carles?"

"He'll be here in a bit. He talking to Gunn about the apartments owned by Ybarra. All the information on those places is in Catalan. He and Caroline are comparing notes and translating for Gunn and Nimesh.

"If we identify the place, we go in hard and fast. Don't shoot at anything unless you're a thousand percent certain who it is. We can't have Layla shot in the crossfire.

That leaves us vulnerable, so we need to be on the top of our game."

Mack thought about getting shot then brushed the thought aside. Since he could remember, baseball taught him that there were times you had to expose yourself to the possibility of injury and not worry about it. He thought of the bunt situation. If a third baseman wanted to make the play, he had to charge the batter. If the batter decided not to bunt but swing away, there was a good chance the ball could nail him between the eyes. That was the risk the third baseman had to take. It was one of the best life lessons baseball taught him: if you want to succeed, be prepared to get smacked in the face then get up and make the play.

Mack asked, "We gotta do what we gotta do." He scratched his head thinking of what they were about to encounter. "Why would J Otis team up with the Otxoa family?"

"We already went over this and didn't have an answer."

"I'm not really looking for an answer. There are two parties, each demanding something different. The Otxoa family wants revenge on Kessler and J Otis wants his money and revenge on me."

"What's your point, Billy?"

"What if Kessler is brought to a different place than where Layla is being kept?"

Garcia wasn't able to answer the question. She climbed out of the dugout and ambled out onto the field.

Mack waited until she was near third base and strolled over to her. "Well? You're the experienced pro.

What do we do?"

Garcia kicked the infield dirt. "At this point, you're asking a hypothetical. We go with what we know. We follow Kessler and react as the situation dictates."

Mack contemplated Garcia's answer. "Trinity and the team in Einsiedeln can run separate tracking and surveillance programs. One can concentrate on Kessler. With his implant he's a given. The other program can concentrate on Jordi Otxoa and Layla. The second tracking is much more difficult. We can't track those two electronically but we may be able to track them with street cams and the satellite, if we're lucky."

"You must have been a Boy Scout growing up."

"Nope, I didn't like their uniforms so I became a baseball player, joined the Little League."

Puyol drove the van along the outer fence of the baseball field, slamming on the brakes when he reached the third base dugout. The van skidded across the grass.

Mack and Garcia jogged over and jumped the short fence. Mack hopped into the front seat and Garcia climbed into the seat behind him.

"I have Kessler's location," Puyol said, holding up his phone screen. "He's five minutes from here, give or take."

The van sped down *Montjuic*, slowing only a little when it hit traffic on the city streets.

~

CHAPTER 31

Kessler sat on the cargo van's bare metal floor with a sack over his head and the drawstring pulled tight around his neck, tight enough that he had difficulty breathing. He felt every bump, every corner, every swerve and counted the time between turns. He didn't panic or fidget. He sat upright. He'd been in this situation before.

He felt the van roll to a stop and heard the van door open and close. It was the van's front passenger door. Over the din of the van's engine, he heard a garage door open. He counted off in his head. Five seconds later, the van coasted a short distance then came to a stop. He heard the garage door roll and close then the door behind him opened. He felt a large hand clamp down on his shoulder and tug.

"You come with me."

Kessler recognized Vlad's voice.

After being helped out of the van, Kessler felt the drawstring around his neck loosen and the black hood was pulled off. He blinked to adjust his eyes. The first thing he saw was Vlad's eyes, too close for comfort.

"Do not move." Vlad said. His hand squeezed Kessler's shoulder.

"Bring that bastard upstairs and get him ready," Nuria ordered. She lit a cigarette and walked through a door and into a sunlit room.

Vlad waited until J Otis went inside before he pushed Kessler through the door. Nuria stood at the windows pulling down the shades so no one could see inside. Vlad twisted Kessler's shoulder, directing him to the stairs on the left.

"As soon as you've secured that fucking executioner in his cell, come back down here. We have a few things to discuss."

As Kessler stepped up on the first stair, Vlad removed his hand. Kessler could feel Vlad on the step below him. Halfway up the stairs, he thought about turning around, bear-hugging Vlad and riding him down the stairs like a sled.

"Stop," Nuria yelled, "and turn around."

Kessler hesitated before he turned. Nuria stood at the bottom of the stairs holding a sawed-off shotgun over her shoulder, her cigarette stuck to her bottom lip. "You try anything and I'll blow you in two."

J Otis cowered. Bewilderment overtook his face.

Sensing the fear in J Otis, Kessler realized it wasn't three against one but two against one. In his business, people like J Otis were only a threat to people on the same team. Kessler dismissed J Otis as a threat.

Vlad pushed Kessler to the top of the stairs and replaced his hand on Kessler shoulder. "Go to door at far end."

Vlad shoved Kessler into a room with hardwood floors and turned on the ceiling light. The glass on the lone window was painted over with red paint.

The room stunk from a mixture of stale blood, sweat and urine.

An old wooden table was pressed against the wall to the left. A large cloth covered the middle of the table. The outlines coming from beneath the cloth looked like a row of medical instruments, lined up largest to smallest.

Leaning against the wall to the right was a rusty wire mattress spring next to a generator with starter cables lying on the floor next to the metal frame. Two ropes hung down with a metal shackle on each end. Two sets of handcuffs were jury-rigged to the bottom of the mattress frame.

Vlad pushed Kessler against the mattress frame and spun him around so they faced each other. "Do not fight, you will lose." Vlad shackled Kessler's right hand then his left. "Move back feet," he said.

Kessler didn't move.

Vlad punched him on the bullet wound in his thigh.

"Move back feet," Vlad said and pulled back his fist. "The crazy woman outside has big fucking gun and she want to use it. Don't give her reason."

Kessler stepped back and braced himself. Vlad attached the handcuffs around his ankles and clamped them tight, digging into his skin.

"Why are you helping her?" Kessler asked, ignoring the pain.

"Is business."

"But, she's about to destroy the life of a sixteen-year old girl. She can take her revenge out on me, fine. But the girl should never have been brought into this."

"She will let girl go after she kill you."

Kessler shook his head vehemently. "No, she won't. She told her psychopath kid he could have her when this was over. I wouldn't do that to my worst enemy." Kessler saw the look on Vlad's face.

Vlad stood face to face with Kessler studying his eyes. “You lie.”

Kessler didn’t move, didn’t blink.

Keeping his eyes locked with Kessler, Vlad reached down and removed the quick-release pin on the shackle around Kessler left wrist. "Don't do anything until I am gone with money." He moved even closer and stood nose to nose. "Or, I come back to kill you."

Vlad walked down the steps with confidence and a smirk.

"I be right back," he said to Nuria.

Vlad walked out to the garage, returned with one Adidas duffel bag and dropped it on the floor. "Here is your share."

"Put it over there," Nuria said, pointing to the corner with the sawed-off shot gun.

Vlad didn't move. "What now you want to discuss?

Hurry because I want to take share and go."

"You haven't finished the job," Nuria said. She flicked her head toward J Otis. "He's still breathing."

"J Otis stepped behind a chair. "What the fuck is she talking about, Vlad?"

"It just business, J Otis," Vlad said. He saw Nuria slowly raise the shotgun and aim it at J Otis, then over to him.

"I don't need either of you anymore. I can eliminate both of you right now."

A wide grin grew on Vlad's face. "If my father does not hear from me in next thirty minutes, the fucking son of you will die slow, painful death then be thrown to pigs for dinner."

Nuria aimed the shotgun at J Otis. "Get the fuck out of here. Both of you."

Nuria cracked open the front door and watched Vlad and J Otis drive away in the van. She waited for a minute to make sure they weren't coming back. She shut the door and locked the deadbolt and the handle.

She figured Jordi realized she wasn’t coming back and was now on the run. He would hole up in the hiding place and call Zigor. She hoped the little bitch wasn’t causing him problems. Nuria wanted to hurt Kessler but only had a short amount of time. He had to be in decent shape when she handed him over to Zigor. She thought about the little bitch. Her desire of one last night with her was surging through her body. Then she’d give her to Jordi.

She strolled into the kitchen and poured herself a

glass of *DYC Whisky*. She slammed down the glass and poured another. She lit a cigarette and finished it in one drag. She dropped the butt in the sink as she exhaled a thick plume of smoke. She wasn't about to allow a coughing fit to erupt.

She carried the glass out to the living area, drank down a large swallow then hurled the glass against the wall. She was ready.

At the top of the stairs, she hesitated to fight off a coughing fit then marched down the hall. She lowered her shoulder into the door, busting it open, hoping to startle Kessler, the executioner.

Kessler grinned at her when she turned to him.

Infuriated, Nuria stomped to the table and whipped off the cloth covering the instruments. She lifted a sharp knife and examined the blade. She cut into the palm of her hand and let a pool of blood form.

She slowly approached Kessler waiting for him to cringe, flinch or start begging.

Kessler sported the same grin.

Nuria wiped the blood in her palm on Kessler's cheek then grabbed his football jersey, sliced it across the front, cutting a large hole.

She ran the blade of the knife across Kessler's stomach, stopped to see his expression then pulled the blade back across his stomach, cutting into Kessler's skin, shallow but deep enough to draw blood.

When she reached the other side, she pushed in the knife a quarter inch and raised her head to see Kessler's reaction.

Kessler's left hand sprung from the loosened shackle

and seized Nuria's throat, choking her. He lifted her off her feet and grinned as her eyes swelled with surprise.

Nuria released the knife but the blade remained stuck in Kessler's side, dangling up and down. The pain was intense but Kessler didn’t react.

She twisted with all her might but couldn't weaken Kessler's grip. She grabbed his forearm with both her hands and tried to push his arm up. He was too strong.

Her lungs began to throb then burn. With her last ounce of strength, she kneed Kessler in the balls.

His grip loosened and she jumped back.

Kessler pulled the knife out and threw it at Nuria, missing over her shoulder.

He reached across and unlatched the shackle around his right wrist. When he bent down to remove the handcuffs around his ankles, he heard a loud commotion coming from over by the table.

~

CHAPTER 32

Puyol parked the van three buildings from the Kessler's location. He twisted in his seat to face Mack and Garcia. "How do you want to play it? The way we discussed or have either of you come up with a better idea?"

Mack kept his eyes glued on the target building.

Garcia said, "We stick to the agreed upon plan that both Layla and John are inside. I go in first acting as if I have the wrong address and finesse my way inside. You two follow once I'm inside."

"I think we should change your plan," Mack said.

"Why is that?" Garcia asked, a touch of sarcasm in her voice. "You have a better idea?"

"Yeah," Mack replied pointing out the windshield

with his chin. "We should split up so we can also follow J Otis and Vlad driving away in that gray Kangoo workman's van."

The door behind Mack popped open and Garcia stepped out onto the street. "You two follow J Otis and the Russian. I will work my way inside and find John." She checked her sidearm, slammed the door and hurried to the target building.

~

Garcia's training kicked in as she marched to the building concentrating on any movement inside or on the periphery.

The old apartment building had two street level doors. The main door was on the far side and close to the garage door. The second door was at the near end.

Garcia walked by in order to inspect the entire building. On the side of the building, the glass of a second story window was painted red. Traces of light peeked through nicks in the paint. A shadow was moving around inside the room.

Garcia walked back, strolling casually past the garage and up to the main door. She stuck her ear against the door and listened. Silence. She dropped to one knee and picked the deadbolt. As she stood, she pushed down on the handle. It didn't budge. She dropped back down to her knee and picked the lock on the handle.

She cracked open the door and listened once again. Silence. She crouched as she pushed open the door and ducked her head into the room. Clear. She slid into the room.

A ruckus up one level caught her attention and she hurried to the stairs. She climbed the stairs with her ears dialed into the ruckus. She kept her pace deliberate. On the top stair, she paused to get a better read. At the end of the hall, a door with its doorframe splintered was cracked open. Garcia readied her silenced pistol in the firing position and glided along the wall.

She kicked open the door.

Nuria Otxoa had a sawed-off shotgun in her hand and was lifting a machete off a wooden table. She turned and raised the shotgun, aiming it across the room.

The shotgun was pointed at Kessler who was on one knee working to undo the handcuff wrapped around his right ankle.

Garcia fired, hitting the shotgun's trigger guard, knocking the snubbed-nosed gun out of Nuria's hand and onto the floor.

Nuria swiveled toward Garcia, raising the machete in her left hand like she's about to throw it.

Garcia fired again. The force of the bullet striking the heel of the machete blade surprised Nuria. The machete fell with its blade down and stuck in Nuria's foot. The handle wobbled back and forth.

Nuria dropped to one knee, looked blankly at Garcia then snatched the handle of the machete and pulled the bloody blade from her foot.

Before Nuria could react, Garcia was on her, ripping the machete from her hand and tossing it aside. She lifted Nuria and carried her over to Kessler.

Kessler quit fidgeting with the handcuffs. He stood, wrapped his arms around Nuria and squeezed the air out of her. It took about a minute before Nuria lost consciousness. Garcia walked over to the table and found a set of handcuff keys. She hurried across the room and unlocked both handcuffs wrapped around Kessler's ankles.

Kessler threw Nuria hard against the wire mattress frame, raised her arms and clamped the shackles around her wrists.

Garcia was on her knees securing the handcuffs around Nuria's ankles. When she finished, she attached the jumper cables to the mattress frame.

"Let's give her a little taste of her own medicine," Garcia said as she reached for the generators on-switch.

"No," Kessler said, "let's tell Vlad's family she made a deal with us to kill Vlad."

Garcia playfully swatted Kessler in the bicep with the back of her hand. "You're thinking and I like that but I have a better idea."

After Garcia explained her plan, Kessler grabbed her and hugged her tight then kissed her hard.

Garcia stepped back. Kessler’s blood was smeared on her shirt. "We'll have time to patch up your wounds later. We have to get to Billy and Carles. They are on their way to find Layla."

Kessler grabbed the towel that was covering the instruments and pressed it against his chest.

~

Mack and Puyol watched J Otis lead Vlad into a three-story townhouse. Hovering behind the brick building were the light fixtures of Camp Nou, the large *fútbol* stadium where Puyol starred for fifteen years. Mack noticed Puyol was concentrating on the windows, unaware of the stadium.

Inside the house, J Otis and Vlad separated. Mack heard yelling through the unit. The voices were audible but neither Mack nor Puyol could make out what they were saying.

Through the windows, J Otis and Vlad reappeared then abruptly stopped and stood about five feet apart, facing each other. They were arguing.

"Let's move now," Mack said. "They definitely won't be expecting us and we get the drop."

"We go from flash to bang," Puyol said and explained his simple plan to Mack. When he finished, he reached below the driver's seat and handed Mack the Smith & Wesson 500 given to him by Garcia.

"Looks like you're flash and I'm bang," Mack said. He readied the stainless steel gun then checked the red-dot site.

"Even with the red-dot site you have to be careful. If Layla is anywhere nearby and your aim is off even by a little, this cannon could blow her apart."

Mack nodded as he took the piece. "If I have to use it, I'll hit at who I'm aiming."

"Where's your weapon?" Mack asked as he opened the van door.

"I'm wearing them."

Mack eyed Puyol up and down. He didn't see any visual evidence, any bulge or even a slight bump to indicate a gun.

Puyol read Mack's eyes. "I don't use firearms. I'm

more effective with blades."

"We have a saying in America. Don't bring-"

"A knife to a gunfight," Puyol interrupted. "I know. Don't worry, I've never been shot and neither have any of my partners. My adversaries, on the other hand, haven't fared too well."

Mack looked Puyol up and down again, trying to figure out where the knives were hidden.

"You can't see them, that's the point. They are behind my back, lower and upper, up my left sleeve and in both pant legs, in case I'm on the ground." Puyol opened the van door. "Let's go get Layla."

~

Through the window, Mack saw J Otis and Vlad still arguing. He gestured for Puyol to get ready.

Mack stood at the front door of the house with his shoulder against the doorjamb. He faced Puyol who was ten feet from the window.

Puyol nodded to Mack and sprinted forward. A foot from the window he jumped and turned his body to hit the glass with his shoulder. The glass shattered around him. He landed in a crouched position, rolled and jumped to his feet, a knife in each hand.

Mack kicked the door open and surged into the room holding the Smith & Wesson cannon in front of him.

J Otis screamed as he jumped back then turned and ran into the kitchen.

Mack fired the Smith & Wesson above J Otis' head, blowing a softball-sized hole in the wall above the door.

J Otis kept running, hitting the kitchen door in full stride flinging it open. He was across the back garden before the door slammed back shut. He jumped the wooden fence and disappeared.

Vlad had Puyol in his sights and raised his Beretta. Before he could aim it, Puyol whipped a knife across the room, burying it deep in Vlad's bicep.

Vlad lowered his pistol, grinned at Puyol and said, "Allow me to remove the knife."

"Place your piece on the floor first."

Mack marched over keeping the cannon pointed at Vlad. "Where's Layla? Where's the girl?"

"I do not know. Our job was to come to here and wait for Neria Otxoa to bring Kessler. She expect me to kill J Otis and give her his money share. My business cruel but I tell to you, I want to be making sure the little girl go free."

Seeing the doubt in Mack's face, Vlad added, "I no care you not believe me. It is truth."

Puyol frisked Vlad then pushed him to his knees. He zip-cuffed Vlad's hands behind his back, pulled out a second zip-cuff and fastened it around his ankles.

"If that's true you may have just saved your life," Puyol said.

Mack headed to the door with his phone in his hand. In all the commotion, he'd received a text message from Trinity. He read the message twice to make sure he understood it.

"Carles, come here. "Jordi Otxoa took Layla and is waiting for a man named Zigor Ybarra to come to him."

Mack tapped the screen on his phone and a map of Barcelona came on the screen. A red arrow pointed to a location over thirty blocks away.

Mack texted Trinity and asked her to send the same message to Kessler and Garcia.

Instantly, he received Trinity's response:

Done. Will keep you updated on new data.

Mack's phone rang while he was reading the message. It was Trinity calling.

"Billy, I have something urgent I do not want to put into a traceable message. Please listen before you ask questions." Trinity paused then said, "Someone in the mayor's office confirmed what Neria Otxoa told Zigor Ybarra, the caller from Pamplona. You and John are wanted by the *Guàrdia Urbana* for the murders of his sons, Xavier and Ignacio. The mayor won't get involved. She doesn't want to risk any blowback that she's protecting foreigners."

"If the *Guàrdia Urbana* has gone public with the warrants for our arrest that means only one thing," Mack said. "The father of the two dead cops wants revenge."

Puyol tossed the van keys to Mack. "Go get Layla. I'll stay here with Vlad in case Otxoa shows up. While I'm waiting, I can find out what he knows. I will also call Gunn and work on getting the warrants rescinded."

"Thanks."

"Wait," Puyol said. "It would be better..."

~

CHAPTER 33

"I got it," Mack said before Puyol finished his sentence and changed his mind, demanding Mack stay while he goes to save Layla.

Before Mack was fully out the door, Vlad contorted himself up into a sitting position. "I tell something else. I also save life of you friend, Kessler. You ask him when he come. When he say I help, you let me go and I take my money share."

"You better pray he is alive," Mack said as he slammed the door behind him.

~

Mack kept a heavy foot on the gas pedal, weaving in between traffic as he passed Camp Nou. He had to drive fast but not draw the attention of the cops. He turned left onto the wide boulevard, *Gran Via de Carles III* and headed north. At the large *El Corte Inglés* department store, he turned right onto *Via Augusta*, saying a prayer as he ran a red light. He kept one eye on the GPS map on his phone while he weaved through traffic. He told himself to be careful but not slow down.

He thought about how he would approach Layla's location. Different scenarios raced through his mind, each more complicated. He decided to keep it simple, direct.

He came to a large roundabout and sped up. He nearly hit a taxi as he entered the roundabout and cursed himself. He shot across traffic, left the roundabout and slammed his foot down on the accelerator. A hundred meters later he came to a smaller roundabout, he stayed on the outside, nearly circling before turning sharply right. He saw signs for *La Sagrada Familia* and slowed. On his left was a long narrow city park. A group of young men and women lined the park playing African Toca Drums; leather-skin drums shaped liked huge wine glasses. The smell of pot seeped into the car.

The rhythmic beat faded as Mack turned away from the park and circled the next block. The GPS indicated he was a half block from his destination.

Parking was only allowed on one side of the street. Mack found an open space. Somebody was watching over him.

He looked at his watch. It was nearly four. The streets were nearly empty as it was lunchtime, the main meal in Barcelona. It would make it tougher for him to approach the location without being noticed.

He counted off the addresses and memorized the front of the target building. He hurried up the street as if he were late getting home for lunch. At the door, he stopped and did a cursory check of the three floors.

He reached down to test the door handle. It was unlocked. He opened the door and strolled in with his right hand behind his back gripping the holstered Smith & Wesson.

The room was starkly furnished. A small, worn red velvet sofa rested under the windows. A large threadbare throw rug covered most of the floor. There was a doorway to what Mack assumed was the kitchen. Across the room was a set of stairs heading up.

Mack floated across the room and stuck his head in and out of the door to the kitchen. It was empty. He entered the kitchen then stopped in his tracks. He cocked his ear and heard a commotion above him.

He pulled the Smith & Wesson from his back holster and readied it as he sidestepped across the room. His hearing perked up as he moved stealthily to the stairs.

He placed his index finger over the trigger guard and silently climbed the stairs trying to pinpoint the origin of the noise as he ascended.

Peering down the hall, he saw a pink door on the left at the far end. Across from the pink door was an identical door but painted red. The noise he'd heard was coming from behind the red door.

Conscious his footfalls could creak on the wooden floor, he walked light-footed to the door and listened.

Behind him, he heard someone clear his throat in a mocking tone. Mack slowly turned around.

A lean, tanned man with gray hair and deep green eyes stepped from behind the pink door pointing an assault rifle at Mack.

"Put your gun on the ground, slowly, then step back." He spoke English with an Irish accent.

Mack didn't move. "Where's Layla?"

The man's eyes glanced at the red door then back at Mack. "Who are you?"

"My name is Billy Mack. Who are you?"

"Where is your partner, the man named Kessler?"

"Who's asking?"

"Since you and Kessler are both dying today, I guess there is no harm in telling you. My name is Zigor, the father of the two men you murdered."

Mack crouched down and laid the large pistol on the floor. He rose cautiously. "You think Kessler and I killed your sons?"

Zigor raised the assault rifle higher. "And you will pay for it."

"Where's Layla?" Mack folded his arms across his chest.

"She's with the boy she'll be spending the rest of her life with. They are getting to know each other."

"You left a sixteen-year old girl with a deranged psychopath?"

"He won't hurt her."

"Bullshit. He's playing with half a deck and it's the wrong half."

"His father and sister were executed by Kessler. She's payback."

Mack dropped his arms and stepped forward so the

barrel of the rifle rested against his chest. "Before you kill me and Kessler, let me set the record straight about your sons. First, your son Xavier was not thrown from his apartment, he jumped through his apartment window because he was about to be exposed as an ETA plant in the *Guàrdia Urbana*. Second, your son Ignacio was already dead when we stumbled upon an army of police outside the place he was killed. The detective in charge said his throat was slit. Funny thing, Kessler wasn't even in Barcelona at the time. He arrived in the early morning after the murders."

"Lies."

"Let's go ask Jordi. See what he tells you. We have time before Kessler arrives. He has the location and is on his way."

Zigor studied Mack. He quickly scratched his cheek with his left hand then clamped it back on the rifle. He pointed the rifle at the red door. "You lead the way."

When Mack grabbed the door handle he heard Layla yell "No. No. No." It took everything he could muster not to shoulder the door open and rush into the room. He twisted the handle and shoved the door open. An ominous feeling washed over him for what he was about to see.

The room was painted deep maroon with a large pink heart painted high up on the wall over the bed. A red light hung down on an exposed wire.

On the bed, Jordi was on top of Layla trying to force himself between her legs. They were both naked and Jordi was panting heavily as he struggled with Layla.

Mack marched over to Jordi knowing there was a

good chance Zigor would shoot him in the back. At the bed, he reached down, grabbed Jordi by the nape of the neck and jerked him off the bed.

Jordi squirmed and moaned as he grabbed the mattress and tried to pull himself back to Layla.

Zigor strolled over, picked up a pair of jeans off the floor and threw them in Jordi's face. "Put these on," he ordered.

Jordi stopped squirming, pulled on the jeans then looked over his shoulder and leered at Layla.

Layla turned away, pulled her legs in and wrapped her arms around her knees. She hid her face in her arms.

Zigor pulled Jordi away from Mack's grip. He bent down, nose to nose and said, "I told you to wait until after Kessler was here."

Jordi glanced at Mack then pointed at him. "Now that Kessler is here, I get to play with her."

Zigor tightened his grip on Jordi's bicep. "Tell me what happened to Nacho."

Jordi's eyes shot left and right then zeroed in on Mack. "Nacho was trying to have sex with my girlfriend when I caught them. After I saved her from Nacho, Kessler..." He pointed at Mack and straightened his arm until it was taut. "This bastard man who killed father and sister, came into the room with a big knife. My girlfriend and I were told to stand in the corner. We were afraid he would kill us. That was when Kessler stabbed Nacho twice, cut his throat then scalped him. Me and my girlfriend ran and hid so he wouldn't kill us. Then we hear Kessler running out and laughing."

Zigor's eyes filled with venom as he snatched Jordi

by the throat. "You sick son of a bitch. You killed Nacho."

"No, uncle Zigor, it was him, Kessler." Jordi jerked free of Zigor, jumped on the bed and lunged at Layla.

Layla was ready. She arched her back and tensed.

With Jordi coming at her, she released her foot.

Mack snatched the barrel of the rifle from Zigor with both hands and jerked the gun from Zigor's hand.

He spun around swinging the gun like a baseball bat. The butt of the rifle landed a crunching wallop in Jordi's temple as Layla's foot zipped past scraping the front of his crotch, missing a direct hit.

Jordi's eyes rolled to the back of his head and he fell sideways, twisted his neck off the corner of the mattress and landed on the hardwood floor. A loud crack echoed through the room. Jordi's head rested at a forty-five degree angle against his shoulder. His breathing was labored. His eyes fluttered and his legs convulsed as he wet himself.

Mack handed the rifle back to Zigor. "What convinced you Jordi killed Nacho?" Mack asked.

"There was no way Nacho was trying to have sex with that girl."

Mack furrowed his brow.

"You don't ask, I won't tell," Zigor said as he reached down and took Jordi by the foot. He dragged him out of the room like a Raggedy Ann doll.

In the hall, Zigor stopped, tossed the rifle into the other room and picked up the Smith & Wesson. "This is now mine," he said then dragged Jordi down the hall.

At the top of the stairs, Zigor said, "You two better leave. If you are here when I get back, I will do to you what I'm about to do to this little shit after I give him his last rites." As Zigor walked down the stairs, Jordi's head bounced off each step.

Mack pulled off his black t-shirt and handed it to Layla. He turned away as she pulled it over her head.

"I always knew you'd come," Layla said.

Mack unshackled Layla's leg and lifted her off the bed. "I'm sorry I missed your birthday party."

She hugged Mack tight and didn't let go.

~

EPILOGUE

Downstairs, Mack kept his arm around Layla's shoulder and held her close. He opened the door and stuck his head out to check the street.

Puyol drove up in the van with Kessler sitting across from him and Garcia in the seat behind. The back door swung open and Mack guided Layla inside. Garcia gave Layla her seat then sat on the van floor next to Mack.

A thundering gunshot rang out from inside the apartment.

Kessler was halfway out the van with his Mossad pistol in his hand when Mack reached up and grabbed his arm.

"Sit back down, John. Some things are better left alone." Mack explained the situation inside and the last words Zigor said to him.

He looked over at Layla to see her reaction. Her eyes were closed and her lips were moving as if in prayer.

"Is that cannon you gave me registered?" Mack asked Garcia.

"Yeah, right," she replied with a snicker. "Why, did you use it or lose it?"

"Neither, it was taken from me... and I think it was just used. I owe you a new one."

"No you don't. I never used it anyway."

Puyol turned the van onto *Via Augusta* and headed up the hill.

"What happened to Neria Otxoa?" Mack asked.

Kessler turned around and looked at Garcia to see who should answer.

Garcia said, "She is wanted in Spain and France for murder, acts of terror and everything that goes with. The French have a much lower tolerance for terrorists. I gave Otxoa's location to an agent who lost a son in a Bordeaux terror attack for which ETA claimed responsibility. I don't think Otxoa will get a welcome reception in France. That is, if she makes it to Bordeaux, which is highly doubtful."

"Why not call the *Guàrdia Urbana*?" Mack asked.

"I made an executive decision," Garcia answered.

"*We* made an executive decision," Kessler said.

"What about Vlad the Impaler?" Mack asked.

All eyes turned to Puyol.

He kept his gaze on the road and pushed down on the accelerator. He weaved through traffic, shot into a left turn lane and stopped.

"I guess I made an executive decision as well."

He turned onto the side street. Two blocks later, he stopped the van in front of the safe house.

"Let's say we have an associate in Moscow to help us find J Otis Weil."

"You let him go?"

"I didn't have much choice. I made a few calls and found out he has diplomatic immunity. He can't come back to Spain, at least not officially."

"You actually think he's going to help us?"

Puyol smiled. "He has a million and a half reasons to be helpful. Besides, I think Vlad is tired or wearing black and would rather wear a white. Isn't that what good guys wear in America?"

"He made it so I could free myself," Kessler said. "When I told him about Otxoa's real plans for Layla, it really seemed to bother him."

"You think he might be helpful if we encounter J Otis again?" Mack asked.

"We'll find out. Gunn is meeting with Vlad tomorrow.

~

Puyol tapped the code into his phone and the steel door to the safe house swung open.

Garcia helped Layla out of the van and took her inside. "We'll get you in the shower then find some clothes that fit. After, I'm taking you shopping."

Mack, Kessler and Puyol meandered into the kitchen. Puyol grabbed three beers from the refrigerator and brought them over to the table.

"To Layla," he said and held up his beer.

Mack and Kessler held up their cans and nodded.

"So John, when are you heading back to Miami?" Mack asked.

Kessler took a mouthful of beer then shook his head and swallowed. "I'm not. I'm moving to Rome. He grinned and took another mouthful.

"You have to look up my uncle when you get there."

"Maite has already spoken to him. We are having dinner next week."

Mack and Puyol leaned back in their chairs and raised their beers.

"Does Ray Gunn know?" Mack asked as he pulled his phone from his pocket. He set the phone on the table and called Gunn.

"Don't say anything," Kessler implored. "I want to tell him at the right time."

"Tell me you have good news," Gunn said, his voice booming out the speaker.

"Layla is safe and getting taken care of by Garcia."

Kessler looked like he just dodged a bullet.

Mack said, "I'll reimburse Vlad's fee to Layla's trust."

"No worries, Billy. The slush fund won't miss it."

"There's one other thing," Mack said.

Kessler tensed, glared at Mack.

"All the kidnappers are dead, or soon to be, except for J Otis. He did a rabbit, again."

"What's new," Gunn said. "I will see what Vlad has to say but finding J Otis is on the backburner right now. I have a bigger fish to catch and fry."

"The mole that gave up Billy and John?" Puyol

asked.

"Correct. It won't take long. In the meantime, Layla needs to go home. Caroline is sending the Aerion back to Barcelona to fly the three of you back to Miami. Carles, you're welcome to join them if you want a beach holiday."

"Thank you but no. I have a waitress I want to get to know." Puyol smiled as he strutted out of the kitchen.

Gunn's voice reverberated through the speaker, "Billy, the firm has decided to open a Miami office. You can work from there while you keep an eye on Layla and make sure she settles back in."

"Miami? Great, who will run the office?"

"Carol Lang." There was pride in Gunn's voice.

"How did you ever get her? She's *thee* player in the southeast. She's kicked our ass on the last three deals."

"I can be persuasive. That and I know her husband Terry. He was very helpful."

"Well done."

"I'm in Miami next week to finalize the deal."

"See you next week," Mack said. He left his phone on the table and went to go check on Layla.

Gunn wasn't done with Kessler. "John, you and I will have a few scotches while I'm in Miami."

Kessler hemmed and hawed, caught himself and said, "Why don't we do that while you're still here in Europe."

There was an uncomfortable silence.

Finally, Gunn said, "Well then, you and Garcia come to Switzerland. We can talk about your move to Rome. My firm will pick up your moving expenses."

"Have you spoken with Maite again?" Kessler asked.

"Call me tomorrow," Gunn replied then hung up.

~

Mack confirmed the flight time back to Miami. As Layla and Garcia headed out to go shopping, Mack handed Garcia a slip of paper with the departure time and the expected time of arrival in Miami. He wanted Layla to call his sister, her mom. It was her first step to getting back to her life.

Up in his room, Mack packed his bags then opened Trinity.

"Congratulations, Billy. I am so happy Layla is safe and sound. It was a pleasure working with you."

"Thank you Trinity. I was my pleasure. How do I get you back to Caroline?"

A video feed opened on the screen with Caroline smiling into the camera. Enrique Iglesias stood behind her. Caroline pointed over her shoulder. "This is my friend Enrique." Iglesias waved as another blonde walked into the picture. "And that's his friend, Anna."

"Nice to meet you," Mack said.

"You as well," Enrique replied. He and Anna waved as they walked away.

The camera centered back on Caroline.

"A job well done, Billy."

"Thank you, Caroline. You were invaluable. I owe you."

"I have more good news. I've identified the man following you in Klosters and to Einsiedeln, the man who died in the BMW. He worked for Gunn at one time. Six months ago, he went rogue. Probably chasing enough money to finance a cushy retirement. I'm convinced he's the mole who gave up you and John. I traced large payments from both Sunden Capital and JOW Holdings into his account in the Bahamas. J Otis must have gotten to him. When we finish here, I'll let Ray know."

Mack filled Caroline in on what ultimately transpired with Zigor and Jordi, Neria, Vlad and, finally, J Otis.

"I'll fill Nimesh in when he gets back from his run."

"One thing I don't understand. I was told Ray Gunn was not involved in the Otxoa operation. Is that true?"

"There was no man *named* Ray Gunn involved."

"Right, *no man named Ray Gunn*" Mack said. "One last thing, how do I get Trinity back to you? I'm taking Layla back to Miami in a couple hours."

"Well then it looks like I'm taking a trip to Miami," Caroline said with a sultry wink. "Since you owe me, you can show me around town. By the way, I love stone crabs."

~

ABOUT THE AUTHOR

Johnny currently resides in St. Paul, Minnesota. He owns Ben Hogan Apex irons he uses as much as he can and an Epiphone guitar he doesn't play anymore. Although he is a Twins fan, he was very happy the Cubs won it all in 2016 (sorry Dave).